THE
Unexpected
GIFT

THE *Unexpected* GIFT

Michelle Bulmer Atha
&
Meaghan Gonzales Wagar

Synergy Books

The Unexpected Gift
Published by Synergy Books
P.O. Box 80107
Austin, Texas 78758

For more information about our books, please write to us, call 512.478.2028, or visit our website at www.synergybooks.net.

Publisher's Cataloging-in-Publication
(Provided by Quality Books, Inc.)

Atha, Michelle Bulmer.
    The unexpected gift / Michelle Bulmer Atha and Meaghan Gonzales Wagar.
    p. cm.
    LCCN 2008910379
    ISBN-13: 978-0-9815462-7-8
    ISBN-10: 0-9815462-7-7

    1. Single mothers--Fiction. 2. Female friendship--Fiction. 3. Georgia--Fiction. I. Wagar, Meaghan Gonzales. II. Title.

PS3601.T43U54 2009   813'.6
                    QBI08-600326

Front Cover Photograph and Design by Brandon Roosa

10 9 8 7 6 5 4 3 2 1

We dedicate this book to every mother, daughter, and sister. Although our paths may vary, our journeys are similar. Give the gift of friendship by inspiring and motivating each other, for your efforts will come full circle.

Chapter 1

It is late autumn in Georgia; the leaves remaining on the trees are vibrant yellow, burnt orange, and ripe red. The air is crisp, bitter at times, yet the season is familiar and refreshing. Why can't I be like fall?

Wait. I am. I am desperately falling apart, and I don't know how to reverse it, or even stop it for that matter. My name is Drew Robbins Warren, and I'm a healthy thirty-eight-year-old woman. Healthy but unhappy. When people look at me, they see my long, auburn hair, piercing green eyes, and olive-colored skin. What they don't see are the emotional scars I bear from having my heart broken.

I do contracted work for an advertisement agency where I used to work full-time before I became a mother. I've been called a task-master, and the level of professionalism I exude is sound. My loving children, Justin and Rachael, are happy, healthy, and seizing life. Yet I still go to bed every night a broken woman, repetitive thoughts of limited opportunities and poor decisions clouding my perception of reality. I wonder, am I sabotaging myself by falling deeper into this depression, or is this just who I really am?

On the bright side, my family is supportive. Although my parents are hundreds of miles away in Virginia, they have always encouraged me to look for the silver lining, to concentrate on Rachael and Justin.

Rachael is my baby; she is nine years old. My daughter is the entertainer of the family; she sings and dances, and she has an innate ability to make anyone laugh. She reminds me of myself when I was a child. Her charisma draws people to her; she seems to spread rays of sunshine everywhere she goes. With her short, blond hair and hazel eyes, she is beautiful inside and out.

My son, Justin, on the other hand, is the strong, silent type. Justin is only eleven years old, and he carries the weight of the world on his shoulders. Justin is the spitting image of his father, and their demeanor is similar. With baby blue eyes, wavy blond hair, and golden-colored skin, Justin looks like he's lived at the beach all of his life. He has a cowlick in the front of his hairline that makes his hair stick straight up, which has made him the envy of many young boys. Justin and his father think outside of the box on most occasions. Their creativity opens doors of opportunity for them in different facets of their lives. I have a special mother-son relationship with Justin; I understand him, especially when others don't.

Then there is Daniel Stephen Warren. He is a successful forty-three-year-old lawyer from Atlanta. I probably made grown women cry the day I took Daniel off the market. When I married him, I knew I was marrying my fairy-tale Prince Charming. He was sophisticated, had gorgeous blue eyes with golden flecks, and thick, wavy, blond hair. He stands just over six feet tall, and he was my protector, my lover, and my best friend. Although I had to use my female persuasions to convince Daniel to have children, he was a great father. It gave me butterflies to think about growing old with him. I wanted to experience everything with Daniel. And I did.

It seems like only yesterday that the phone rang and my world fell apart. Kelly, my best friend, was distraught and confused. She gave me the heartrending news. She started by asking if Daniel was home. I told her no. It was a ridiculous question. Daniel woke up and left for his law firm at the same time every morning; he's the most consistent person I know. Kelly then explained that she needed to tell me something, friend to friend. I began to worry; I feared Daniel had been in a horrible accident. I told Kelly to calm down because she was scaring me. Then she began to cry and told me how she had seen Daniel entertaining a young, blond woman at Cedars Restaurant one evening. A client, I presumed. Kelly then explained how she had watched Daniel walk the woman to the car, lean up against her, and kiss her passionately. Kelly said that as she stood in shock and watched the girl drive away, Daniel turned, made eye contact, gave her a smirk, and walked past her to reunite with some buddies at the bar. As I heard Kelly speaking, I felt a sharp pain in my stomach. I felt so weak in the knees, I fell to the floor, and my life source drained away. There was silence on the phone for what felt like an eternity. I told Kelly I had to go, and she whispered, through her sobbing, that she was sorry. I hung up the phone, but it rang again immediately; it was Daniel. He sounded like a stranger as he said he wouldn't be home for dinner because he had a late appointment with a client, again. My heart sank even lower.

As I lied in bed, months later, replaying memories from the not-so-distant past, I knew I had to get up. I dragged myself to the bathroom and looked into the mirror. I didn't recognize myself anymore. Sleepless nights, restless days, wrinkles, and swollen eyes—how did this happen to me? Once a beautiful woman, envied by others, I now lived in shame and despair. After fourteen years of marriage to the man of my dreams, I faced the world alone, and I couldn't seem to grasp any means of control. It made me sick to think that the man who once told me he never wanted children because they would drain the love we had for each other, had taken my—our—children away for yet another weekend.

Feeling like I had failed as a wife, I concentrated solely on my role as a mother, so when my children were with Daniel, I did not know what to do with myself. I could hear Daniel now: "You have your dream home, the Mercedes, the lake house, and no financial burden." But what I really had were shattered dreams. I was left with the burden of facing the reality of what my life had become. Dream home? The dream had been to make this house a home with our family and the love we shared. That dream was now a nightmare; it was empty, cold, and lonely, just like me.

The phone snapped me out of a daze; Rachael was calling to tell me they would be home in a few hours. I realized I needed to get myself together, for their sake—another acting job. I deserved an Academy Award for the number of times I had put on a brave face over the past few months, while I tucked my children into bed and told them everything was going to work out for the best, or while they raved about the camping and hiking trips they took with their father and Julie, the twenty-two-year-old receptionist. If they only knew how I was really feeling inside, the devastation and betrayal I feel at the hands of the person who was supposed to love me forever. I was once a woman who had it all, living the American dream, and suddenly I live moment to moment, and I feel my world is crumbling more and more each day.

The children were going to be home soon, and I was neurotic about looking my best whenever there was a chance I would see Daniel or Julie. I never wanted to give Daniel any justification for leaving me—for instance, because he thought I'd let myself go or that I wasn't attractive anymore. I always wanted him to see me at my best, not the ugly mess I had become. Inevitably, when I knew I was going to see him, I took a bath, dried and styled my hair, applied fresh makeup, and wore his favorite perfume. The production was like getting ready for the prom, every time. But it was worth it to me because, as horrible as I felt inside, I wanted to look happy and pretty for Rachael and Justin. I didn't want them to suffer by worrying about me.

I continuously peeked between the blinds in the living room, watching for Daniel's car to turn the corner, as I had on so many occasions when Daniel worked late. I was excited to see my children, but dreaded hearing about their weekend. Daniel was such a charmer; he could make a snake do the two-step.

"Yes, thank you, God!" My stomach dropped as I saw his sleek, black Jaguar slowly turn the corner. My babies were home! I didn't want them to know I was desperately waiting by the window, so I ran into the family room, turned the television on, and sat on the couch. I collected all of my energy in order to paint on a Stepford smile and begin the show.

I heard the door chime, and Rachael's voice called, "Mommy, we're home!"

I gracefully walked into the foyer, and said, "I'm so happy to see you!" I then gave them each a hug as if I had not seen them in a hundred years.

Daniel looked at me, then turned his head and told the kids to run upstairs so he could talk with me. He gave the kids a quick kiss on their foreheads and told them good-bye. I felt nervous. I am a grown woman, yet there was something about Daniel that made me feel inferior. I mean, when he and I were together, I had liked him being the strong, dominant partner, but since we were not on the same team any longer, I felt intimidated by his overwhelming sense of self-confidence.

Usually, when Daniel speaks, he controls the conversation by making demands, rather than requests; he never feels the need to speak defensively or back up his demands with any kind of excuse or reason. I really had no idea what he was going to confront me with, so I waited for him to speak first.

"Drew, I've made reservations for Julie and me to spend the first week of February with the kids, skiing in Colorado. We'll be staying at the Old-Farm Mountain Resort. I will provide you with all of the details after the first of the year, a little closer to the trip."

My heart was pounding; I was speechless and hurt. Had Daniel already forgotten that my birthday was on February sixth? I didn't want to rock the boat, so I told him I would think about it.

"What's to think about? Are you going to deny our children a skiing trip with their father?"

"No, Daniel, that's not what I'm saying." I sure wasn't going to remind him that my birthday fell during the first week of February. "It's just that I have already made plans for the children and myself during that same week." The children and I have always shared my birthday together. It's tradition for Rachael and me to bake my birthday cake after a family dinner, and then for all of us to sit and watch home videos of birthdays past. How could Daniel forget those special times? I wanted to tell him no right away, but I didn't want to disappoint the children. I could see the excitement on their faces when they had walked through the door, and now I knew it was because of the trip: perhaps I would muster up the nerve to discuss this with him later.

"Drew, the reservations have been made. I am expecting to take the children to Colorado, February first through February seventh."

Daniel is a selfish, self-centered soul. He wants what he wants, and there is no bargaining. He turned toward the door and walked away. As he left, I watched for a second, then Julie caught my eye. She had been sitting in the car the whole time. What a coward. I wanted to take the high road and just close the door, but I couldn't. I waved obnoxiously to Little Miss Julie as she sat in the front seat of the car that I used to ride to church in on Sundays. She waved back as if she were caught or confused. Then they drove away.

I still couldn't believe my life had come to this point. Would every other weekend repeat this same exhausting routine? I realized I needed to snap out of it and enjoy the time I had with my children before they left me again. The time went by so quickly that I felt like I was living my life based on my custodial weeks and weekends; when I made plans, my first thought was to determine whether it was my weekend with my children or not. I guessed this was what I would have to face for many years to come.

I made my way upstairs to join the kids. The show must go on. I prepared myself as I took each step closer to hearing all of the glorious details of their adventurous weekend with their father and Julie.

As I walked into Rachael's room, I saw her opening the small box of chocolates I'd picked up for her while she was away. I had gotten in the habit of buying small gifts for Rachael and Justin on the weekends when they were with their father as a way of letting them know I was thinking about them. I left their surprises on their beds. In a way, I think I subconsciously also wanted to ensure they would be excited to come home, especially after the fun-filled weekends they had with their dad. Although admitting it sounded desperate, I couldn't face the idea of the children not wanting me. Daniel had loved me unconditionally, or so I thought, yet I was easily replaced. I couldn't bear the thought of that happening with the children.

"Hey, honey, I missed you! How was your weekend?" I really didn't want to know the specifics, but as a loving mother, I showed interest in all of the aspects of my children's lives, even the ones that broke my heart.

Just then, Justin came into the room, put his arms around my neck, and told me that he loved me. He thanked me for the baseball cards I'd left on his bed, and joined us to talk about their weekend. As Rachael began to tell me all the details, I could hear in her voice how much she loved being with her father. Justin chimed in sparingly, but I saw in his eyes the love he, too, had for his father. I knew that Justin was trying to suppress his excitement in order to spare my feelings. He has always been intuitive of others' feelings, a trait he inherited from me.

Listening to the children's details, I acknowledged that this would be an adjustment I would have to deal with over time. That thought overwhelmed me. At that moment, I decided to take it day by day. I would embrace and work through this adjustment and realize it was a new beginning for the children as well. It was a reality I simply had to accept.

Chapter 2

As I lied in bed, tossing and turning, I began dreaming. Sounds of a train running over the tracks comfort me in my sleep. Little flashes of familiar sights while I was looking out of the train window flit through my mind as I slip into the deep stage of my sleep. I saw myself as a pretty little girl, around the age of seven, hugging a gentle, older man. "I love you, Daddy," I said as we held on to each other tightly. Suddenly, the dream switches to a nightmare. A force rips me out of my daddy's arms. We both reach our arms out toward each other as I scream out in terror, "Daddy!"

I woke myself up screaming. I came to a sitting position, heart racing and dripping with sweat. Realizing that this was all a dream, I had a sense of relief. Looking at my surroundings, the dark, blank walls, the cold cement floors, I lied back down and began to think about the past. When are those kinds of dreams going to go away? They were a thing of the past, or so I thought.

The dreams brought back memories of elementary school, drawing pictures with a stick in a sandbox in the school counselor's office many years ago after speaking to my teacher about the nightmares. The nightmares about my father and how our lives were torn apart began when I was in the second grade. Granny would often come in and tell me to go back to sleep, shutting the door tightly. Luckily, I was a precocious little girl who loved to tell stories. My teacher, Mrs. Little, was so kindhearted. She gave me the courage to speak my mind. She was the one who sent me directly to our counselor, Mrs. Baker.

"These dreams are all a part of the things that have happened to you," Mrs. Baker would say with a sympathetic expression on her face. "Your mind has to let go of some of the sadness and anger. These dreams are how your feelings come out," she reassured me. "It is perfectly normal."

I loved going to the counselor's office. It made me feel important. Someone was actually interested in what I had to say. I was always grateful to my teachers, as well, for allowing me to go when I needed to. The truth is, I would much rather speak to the teacher or the counselor than my grandmother.

"We all got problems, Leah," Granny would say. "You just need to keep moving on as I do."

The truth of the matter is that Granny was not a loving and caring grandmother at all. I used to read stories in school about grandmothers and how sweet and understanding they were. "Not mine," I would say to the counselor. "My grandmother was more like the wolf in that story *Little Red Riding Hood* that dressed up like a grandmother. Sure, she wore the costume well, but underneath it all, she was a mean old wolf."

I can remember many visits from the social workers to my home after that meeting with Mrs. Baker. Granny would have lots of interviews and lectures about how to be more loving and patient. This only made Granny more distant. Instead of yelling at me, she just stopped speaking to me altogether. I didn't know which form of abuse was worse.

I decided to get out of bed and get ready for work. Although I'm a pregnant eighteen-year-old girl, living on my own, I'm not lonely. My place is dark and dreary, but it's mine. I had a talent for sewing, or so friends would tell me. The sewing machine and the talent were the only positive things I inherited from Granny. I took scraps I'd gotten from fabric stores that were throwing them away and turned them into cute curtains, tablecloths, and even handbags. I sometimes made handbags for people that I work with at The Family Dinner. I really don't care much for my job, but I like the fact that I live close and I can walk. It gets me out of my apartment for a few hours and gives me some money for the week. I don't need much. I have my granny's old furniture after her passing, and my apartment is what they call government-subsidized based on my income. I oftentimes hear fighting and late night partying in the apartments around me, but this is no different than my childhood home. My mama was an alcoholic who moved me and her in with Granny as a baby. My mama often had different men in and out and friends over all hours of the night. This would drive Granny crazy, and fights would break out between Mama and Granny, sometimes ending in a visit from the police. I would lie in bed, pretending to sleep, but listening to all that was going on. From a very young age, I realized that I would much rather be alone than with people who hated each other.

Getting out of the shower, I stopped in front of the mirror and examined my belly.

"Not any bigger yet," I said to myself.

I went into the kitchen to fix two bowls of oatmeal before going to work. One for me and one for my neighbor next door.

She was a sweet, older, black woman named Gladys. I sometimes brought her food, either homemade or taken home from the diner after work. Gladys often brings me material that she has gathered up to help me sew. We have become really close and check in on each other quite a bit. Pouring the oatmeal into two bowls and sprinkling a bit of brown sugar on the top, I walked next door to share.

"Knock, knock," I said, as I stood close to Gladys's door instead of actually knocking.

"Oh, Leah, dear," Gladys said as she opened the door and smelled the wonderful aroma of breakfast. "How kind of you. Come in, come in."

"Well, I can't stay long, I need to get on to work, but I just knew you would be crazy enough to be up this early," I said sarcastically.

"I have been up for a bit, I reckon," Gladys said. "What you got going on today, Leah?"

"Oh, not much. I figure after work, I may just come back and take a nap. Didn't sleep so well last night. I kept having weird dreams."

"That is a true sign you is having a baby, Leah," Gladys said frankly. "All pregnant women have weird dreams."

"Yes, it's just that I used to have these same dreams as young girl, but they went away a bit as I got older. That is until now. I keep dreaming about my daddy. It's so strange."

Gladys reached out and touched my arm. "I am so sorry, dear. Do you reckon you'll ever see him again? Maybe this is a sign that good things are yet to come."

"Well, ever since Mama and Granny died, I don't have connections to any family. I wouldn't even know how to try to find him. He may be dead, too, for all I know. I just think that even trying to find him would just open up all those old family memories that I don't really want to relive," I said honestly.

Meeting my father again would be just too much right now. My boyfriend Rick thinks that I don't need to try and find someone who doesn't want anything to do with me anyway. Rick thinks my daddy is probably dead, and my dreams are just my imagination running wild. I don't know what he would think if I actually wanted to meet him again. I am trying to keep things going good with Rick right now. I am hoping our baby is going to bring us closer together.

"Have you talked to Rick about all of this?" Gladys asked. "That's what a boyfriend is for ,you know, to help you through things."

"No, he wouldn't understand. I have tried to talk to him before about the past, and he just tells me he doesn't have time for more problems. He's worried enough about the future."

"Leah, I have told you before, and I will tell you again, that man is no good for you. Why I saw him just yesterday driving in his pickup truck with a young girl, and it just ain't right! I hope you are through with him and his rages! Has he laid a hand on you lately?" Gladys asked with great concern.

"No, actually he said that he won't do anything that would hurt the baby. He has me convinced of that," I said.

"Baby or no baby, he has no right to put his hands on you. If I wasn't so old and frail, I would whoop him myself!" Gladys said in a very angry voice.

I let out a great big burst of laughter and said, "I bet you would, Gladys, I bet you would. Now, off I go. I will see you when I get home from work." I stood and gave Gladys a kiss on the top of her head and headed for the door.

"Thank you, Leah. I'll get the dishes and lock up for you. You just go on ahead."

I began my short walk to the diner. My job is simple. Clean the bathrooms, empty the trash, and mop up the floors. I have been working there ever since I finished high school. Granny had died two years before I graduated, so I moved in with Rick. It was either that or go and stay in some foster home. Rick said he would take care of me. I told the people at school he was my uncle so I didn't get taken away. He actually let me stay at his place for free as long as I was there to clean and help cook dinner and stuff. Some people would think it was weird that I date someone who is more than ten years older than me, but the truth is I have always gotten along with people older than me. They seem to have problems more like mine. I never had time just to sit and play or talk on the phone like a normal kid. I was always helping with the cooking, cleaning, and finding ways to make extra money. I was proud of myself for finishing school and getting my diploma. I was always pretty good at schoolwork. They would put me in the smaller classes, but I could always keep up and get good grades. I was the first person in my family to graduate. Nobody came to see me get my diploma that day, seeing as how Granny and Mama had already died, and Rick had to work. But I was doing just fine inside. It was one of the happiest days of my life. I even got a card with money in it from my old counselor Mrs. Baker. She was retired then but said she was still thinking of me. It gave me strength. This actually made me feel strong enough to live on my own and to keep working hard.

I moved out of Rick's place a few months ago. He got more and more violent, and he just felt that we would get along better when I moved out. I actually agreed. There are things I miss about living with him. I loved the smell of his skin when I would lie close to him. It had a familiar smell of something sweet. I couldn't quite put my finger on it. It was just familiar and comfortable. I remember smelling that same smell from Robbie Curtis, the boy who sat in front of me in my math class in high school. He was so cute: a real jock. I guess that is why he was in the slower classes like me. School wasn't the most important thing on our minds. He was playing ball; I was trying to survive. He was always really nice to me, too. I would let him copy my homework, and he would tell me funny jokes and stuff. I knew he would never like a girl like me, but I loved the attention. His cute red hair and freckly face gave me butterflies in my stomach. And that smell of his skin—I can still remember the exact smell. He would lean in real close to copy my work, and I would secretly breathe the sent that was escaping from his shoulders. It would make me forget all of my problems for those few minutes. He would even say "Hey" to me when we would pass in the hallway. Even when he was with the cooler kids, it didn't matter to him. He went out of his way to notice me. There were even times when Rick would head out to the bars on a Friday night, and I would have him drop me off at the high school to catch the football game. I would get to watch Robbie in action. I was there alone, so I would just stand in a place where no one could see me and pretend that I was there to see my boyfriend and that he knew I was there for him. Pretty sad, I know, but dreams are sometimes all that kept me going. There was one time Robbie caught the ball and ran down for a touchdown. Everyone was cheering. He seemed to stop and look around for somebody. I like to think he was looking for me.

I would call Rick to pick me up, and he would often show up an hour after the game was over or whenever he was ready, so I would just sit and wait alone in the bleachers at dark. But it was all worth it. Any time spent watching Robbie was worth it. Sometimes when I would go back home and get into bed, I would think about Robbie and the smell of his shirt. It would help me face what I needed to do to keep Rick happy. Now Robbie is probably off at some expensive college with my other classmates, while I'm here, pregnant, working at the diner. But at least I have those memories. And I also have Rick to thank for helping me in my times of struggle. I only wish he made me feel like I did when Robbie looked at me. I wonder what he would think if he knew I was having a baby. I wonder if he thinks of me at all. But those things aren't really supposed to happen to a girl like me. It is just not "in the cards" as Granny would say. "Be happy with what you have." I have myself, Rick, and the baby.

Rick did save me from a lot of heartache, but he also caused me more heartache than a person should have to bear. I knew there was someone better out there, but I had no way of finding him. Rick was the only man I have ever laid in bed with. I wasn't going to be like Mama and have different men all the time. I was going to meet one and stick with him, no matter how bad it got. And sometimes it got real bad. That is why I love having my job. It was at least a step toward being my own person. The owners are kind people who sometimes slip me an extra twenty here and there. Every bit helps.

"I wish we could do more," they would often tell me.

"Don't worry about me," I tell them, "I'm fine."

And I was telling the truth. I am fine. My life may seem boring or even sad to some, but I am mostly happy. Oh, sure, there are still dreams. Dreams of me and my baby having a happy family and a home. But for now, I just make the choice to keep living. There are many days and nights when I find myself crying. Sometimes it just starts happening for no good reason. I guess the fact that Rick doesn't come around often makes me feel a bit depressed. I do miss having someone around. Even if we weren't talking much. I still liked having him near. I know Gladys is right, and I can't trust him. The only person I can really trust is myself. I just need to try to stay happy for the baby's sake. As long as I can stay busy, and my baby is healthy, things are good.

"I have one thing that no one can ever take away from me," I would tell people around me, "and that is my dreams. Dreams for better things still to come." Even though my life sometimes seems hopeless, I was born with the ability to look at the positive side of life, or so my teachers would say. I was always searching for something better. This was my dream.

Chapter 3

A new beginning: ugh, I hate that phrase. Every time I mentioned my divorce to people, they gave that disconcerted smile and said, "Well, look at this as a new beginning." In reality, divorce is not a beginning. It is the end of a life that was built over years of love, trust, and familiarity. The thought of starting over for me was sad, a pathetic place to be. As for Daniel, his "new beginning" seemed to be one of excitement and adventure. What did he have to lose? He had his career, his children on a convenient, every-other-weekend arrangement and of course his new girlfriend, Julie.

When he first admitted to me who she was and that he was in love with her, I almost wanted to laugh. "A receptionist?" I asked. "Damn, Daniel, what happened to 'I can only love an educated, self-sufficient woman'?" A woman like me. It was just another lie on his list of betrayals.

I tried to occupy my time by staying busy. But there seemed to be reminders everywhere. One afternoon, as I stood in the checkout line at the grocery store, I faintly heard a man and woman laughing. I casually turned to look at them, my mind flooding with memories of Daniel and me finding humor in little things. The couple was young, and they looked so happy. I wanted to be happy, but instead I was angry. I wanted a man to love me again. What I really wanted was for Daniel to take me back and love me forever, the way he'd promised he would. I reminded myself to stay focused; I needed to concentrate on what I had now: my two safe, wonderful children, whom I loved unconditionally. Unconditional love…can unconditional love exist between a man and a woman forever? I didn't know all of the answers; I needed time to mend.

This experience, the divorce, had made me realize how superficial people can be. Women I thought were friends showed their true colors when the going got rough, and they got going. When Daniel and I were married, I was a regular at the neighborhood ladies Bunco night. I was the alternate tennis partner who filled in on what seemed like every weekend. But now, when I needed my friends the most, they were nowhere to be found. They had abandoned me. If the ladies wanted to ignore or neglect their friendship with me, I could accept that. But what I couldn't accept were the cruel words they used behind my back, which passed through the grapevine and landed on my children's ears.

Just a few days before, I had watched Rachael and Justin get off the bus. Normally Justin strolled along toward the door and Rachael moved with a little more enthusiasm; she's energetic, excited to be home. This day was different. I saw Justin shout back at the bus, and then quickly turn to catch up with his sister. Rachael was walking up the driveway with slumped shoulders and her head held low; she had been crying. I would never have imagined why, had I not been told.

As Rachael had come in the house, she'd thrown her book bag down and run up the stairs. I stood speechless. Justin followed her in and came toward me. "What's going on?" I'd asked.

"Rachael's friends were teasing us about Dad."

"What about your dad?"

"You know, how Dad has a new, younger girlfriend than you," he muttered, staring at the floor.

"Who was saying this?" As Justin began to tell me the names of the girls on the bus, I realized they were the daughters of the women I once played tennis and cards with, and with whom I'd shared laughter and enjoyed other family events. Now not only had they turned against me, but they'd turned their children against mine.

I hugged Justin, put on a brave front, and told him that everything was going to be okay. I told him that time heals all wounds, that something else was bound to happen in this community, and then our family's business would no longer be the talk of the town. I told Justin to go into the kitchen to eat a snack while I talked with Rachael.

As I sat on Rachael's bed, I told her, "Every family experiences change. We are no different than anybody else. Our change was the divorce, and we will continue to work through this as a family. We have not been beaten down. One thing I can share with you that I've especially learned lately is that true friends will not hurt you—they'll support you. Anybody who is willing to spread rumors is not a good person or your friend." I told Rachael that she was a spectacular person, and that she needed to surround herself with positive people. This was a new beginning for all of us, a fresh start.

Rachael and I joined Justin in the kitchen. This disaster ended up opening a door of communication for us to discuss how we felt about our new life. It needed to happen, and the advice I gave to Rachael was also advice I needed to hear for myself. It's funny—we think we are our children's teachers, but in reality, they end up teaching us. If only I had the inner strength to verbally confront those women; instead, I continue to hope that things will get better in time.

Time was passing slowly. I made the decision that if I had to look at my life as a new beginning, I would start with the house. The next time Daniel picked the children up, I went straight to work throwing away old reminders of Daniel's and my past. It was empowering to discard old cards, photos, and little notes we'd shared and I'd saved over the years. Things that were all painful realities of past promises made that were now broken and disposed of. I even threw away our premium fifteen-hundred-dollar wedding album. The evidence of all of the garbage he fed me now lay in the trash. As I glanced over at the white satin, pearl-covered album lying in the trash, I noticed that it was next to chicken bones and wadded-up napkins. I realized that they all had the same value: nothing. They were worthless.

I did save the photos of us with the kids; I knew Rachael and Justin would want them someday. The hardest part was when I came across the boxes of baby items. Clothes, shoes, and toys I had saved for sentimental reasons, and for the secret hope that perhaps one day, Daniel and I would be surprised with another baby. I love being a mother, and having another child was always in the back of my mind. Now I realized how important it would be for me to get rid of these items. I needed to do it for my own sanity. I just hated to throw them away, or to donate them someplace, not knowing if the people receiving them would cherish them the way I had. I held special memories of each piece. I wished I knew someone who was expecting and would treasure the baby things, but all of my friends' children were grown.

I felt like I was on autopilot, on a mission. I began to pack all of the baby items in newer, sturdier boxes. After loading them into the trunk of my car, I decided to donate them in a needier part of town. That way, I figured, any expectant mothers living in the area would be pleasantly surprised by the gently used treasures. I just needed to hold onto my own memories and hope that whoever used these items next would make wonderful memories for themselves. But more importantly, dropping these boxes off would at least give me a reason to get out of the house while the children were with their father.

I drove down a one-way road in one of the poorer neighborhoods and found myself stopped at a red light. Looking to the left, I noticed a small circle of houses we often called "the projects"; it was a government-assisted residence. I watched people walking around the parking lot. There were some adults hanging out in the parking lot area, and unkempt kids running around with what looked like old clothes and extremely worn shoes. It was the end of November, but there wasn't a child in sight wearing a coat, or even a jacket. I was reminded of how Daniel despised people less fortunate than we were. Daniel had protested when the plans were being made to build these particular homes. He was adamant about keeping the underprivileged away from our community and especially our children. He firmly believed that people in lower socioeconomic classes were there only by choice, and he often referred to them as the "societal sloths."

As the light turned green, I hesitated. The donation center was straight ahead, but something inside me wanted to turn left. Was I driven by the desire to rebel against Daniel's ignorant views? Perhaps. But it also felt empowering to make a decision for myself, and not to allow Daniel's influence to determine my destiny. What if there was a woman there who was down on her luck and expecting a baby? And what if she didn't have some of the extras, or even the necessities? Daniel would be furious if he knew I was contemplating giving our children's hand-me-downs to a "societal sloth."

A car behind me honked its horn, startling me out of my deliberations. I turned left. I was nervous; I had never been here before and felt scared being out of my element. I made sure my doors were locked, hid behind my sunglasses, and was thankful that my Mercedes had tinted windows. I wasn't embarrassed to be there; I just didn't know how to act. I was a sheltered woman, but something inside gave me the courage to continue to drive. I heard some shouting; there were about six or seven men, probably in their twenties or thirties, smoking on a front porch, laughing and carrying on as I drove past. I ignored them.

And then, like a beacon of light, I saw a pale young woman sitting alone on what I assumed was her porch. She looked pregnant. She looked like what some people refer to as "white trash." A part of me thought there was no way I could hand over my precious things to someone so grim, so rough-looking. But as I drove closer, I could tell she had been crying; her face was covered with red splotches. The pain in her eyes overwhelmed me. I wondered if she had been crying all night, as I had. I wondered if she had been crying because of a man, too. We were different from each other, yet could the feelings of pain be the same? She looked at me, and, unbelievably, I felt a connection. It felt as though she was waiting for me, or that we were supposed to meet somehow. I'm a spiritual person, but I was experiencing unfamiliar emotions.

I pulled the car over and began to roll the window down, not knowing how I would address the young girl. To my surprise, the girl stood up as my car came to a halt, and before I could even speak, she addressed me.

"Let me guess—you're lost," the girl said, with a smirk on her face.

"Um, actually, I saw you sitting here and noticed you looked like you're expecting. I have some baby items to give away. Are you interested? Nothing is new anymore, but everything is quite nice: gently used clothes, shoes, baby sheets, towels, and toys."

"Sure, I'll take anything if it's free."

I popped the trunk. The girl immediately began to attempt to retrieve the boxes. I sat in my car, watching her through my rearview mirror; she was struggling. I hadn't planned on getting out of the car, but I couldn't sit and watch a young pregnant girl strain herself.

All of a sudden, I heard a bit of a hoarse-sounding, older voice, coming from the porch next door. "Leah, baby, you need some help?"

The girl, who seemed like a lost soul, had a name: Leah.

Leah shouted back, "Getting some baby stuff. You go on in, it's too cold out here for you. I'll come by and show you later."

At this point, I found myself getting out of the car, lifting a box, and walking toward Leah's duplex. As I stepped over the threshold, the stench of stale, damp air overwhelmed me. I was taken aback by the odor; it reminded me of my grandmother's basement after it had flooded. And Leah was living in this environment. I then noticed the drab color of the walls. It was like a jail cell. The place was not dirty, per se; it was just lifeless. I found it ironic since she would soon give life. There were hints of cheerfulness in what looked like homemade curtains and doilies.

After the last box was brought in, I didn't know what to do. Leah began to open one of the boxes. I asked her, "Are you having a boy or a girl?"

"Oh, I don't know. I haven't been to the doctor yet. Rick, my boyfriend, is going to take me, but he's been busy, looking for a job and stuff."

"What about your parents? Couldn't they take you?"

"I haven't got any."

Taken aback by such a dreary situation, I realized how badly this young girl must need my baby things. Still, I wasn't emotionally prepared to get to know this unfortunate girl and to be informed of her sad life. I decided it was time to leave. I wished Leah the best of luck and told her to enjoy the items, thinking I would never see her again.

Little did I know I would be haunted by thoughts of Leah and concerned about her living situation. Although I had my own children and myself to worry about, I couldn't help but think about Leah. It was almost, in a sad way, a good distraction from my own personal depression. Leah's problems appeared to have a potentially detrimental effect on her unborn baby's life, as well as her own, and my problems, in comparison, were more manageable. These thoughts kept me up at night.

Chapter 4

As if Christmas had arrived early, I closed the door to my duplex and immediately began unpacking the boxes of baby gifts. Referring to them as gifts was accurate; I knew the odds of my being thrown a baby shower were minimal. Touching and smelling every piece of baby clothing, I embraced the thoughts of innocence and new life. Promising to make a better life for my baby, I was determined to do everything right and take responsibility for my bundle of joy.

The phone rang. Rick was calling. I had been part of Rick's three-ring circus for almost two years, indulging in his every whim. The third party was whatever other girl would put up with Rick's drunken, abusive behaviors—on a temporary basis, of course.

In the beginning of our relationship, we were inseparable. Although Rick never fostered a strong work ethic, he seemed to pay the bills and still have money left over to party. Considering I was only sixteen when we met, I fell head over heels in love. Rick had been in several more relationships than I could ever imagine, so he took full advantage of having a much younger girlfriend when the time came. The honeymoon period was short-lived. The whirlwind ended after just five months. Rick began to grow tired of feeling obligated to bring me along or to pay my way. I didn't lose hope in our relationship, though. It became second nature for me to come up with excuses for Rick not being around or for times when he would pick fights with me. In fact, I was becoming such a master at covering up for Rick, or lying to defend him, that I could probably spit out reasons for his transgressions before he even committed them.

I wanted to stay with Rick because I was in love with him. I admit Rick had some problems, but I felt like I could change him, help him to do better and feel better. Rick had had some rough breaks in life, and I wanted to right the wrongs for him and make life better. But Rick's agenda differed from mine. A noncommittal man, moving from one woman to the next, living like a nomad, Rick didn't want to settle down and live the American dream. As long as he had a full belly and a beer in hand, he was a satisfied man. His temper flared often, but I took it in stride. From time to time, when Rick would push or slap me around, I blamed myself for pressuring Rick to meet overly high expectations, or I'd figure that he was under a lot of stress and I should've been able to relieve some of that for him. But over time, I began to be desensitized to the lifestyle I was living. I accepted my future with an inconsistent man who rarely showed me peaceful, loving moments. It appeared to be my destiny.

When I discovered I was pregnant, I thought that Rick and I would share in the joy together. This was not the case. Rick wanted no part of it. Coming home after a long day, Rick just wanted to pop open a cold one and watch television in a semi-comatose state. I tried cozying up to him on the couch so I could tell him the good news, but he wasn't in the cozying mood. I remember that morning like it was yesterday. I'd timed my pregnancy test by the clock on the microwave. It felt like the longest three minutes I ever spent. Tears of joy rolled down my face when I saw those two bars inside that window. I hadn't ever been so excited for something: a new beginning. I couldn't think about anything else the rest of the day. I couldn't wait to tell Rick he was going to be a daddy.

When I saw that Rick wasn't going to be showing me any affection, I went and got the pregnancy test. I handed it to him. With his eyes fixated on the football game, he held that test in the palm of his hands for what seemed like forever. Finally, at a commercial, he looked to see what he was holding. I couldn't wait to see his reaction.

At the top of his lungs, he shouted, "What in the hell is this?"

"Rick—Rick, we made a baby."

"Oh, no, *we* did not make a baby. You did this. This is your fault. This is your mistake."

Confused by Rick's reaction, I burst into tears. My dream, my salvation, my baby angel, this baby was no mistake. This baby was my future, and I was its future. Rick stormed out. He didn't even come home that night. I stayed awake worrying about him, falling asleep around four a.m. I was tired, but I knew Rick had only overreacted because he was probably worried about having another mouth to feed.

Three days went by, with no phone call or any other contact, before Rick came home. I had been feeling nauseated, so when I wasn't upset over Rick, I was lying in the bed thinking I was going to be sick. At this point, I figured I was probably about six or seven weeks pregnant. I knew I should start thinking about going to a doctor, but I was making sure I was taking care of myself in the meantime. I knew Rick would take me once things calmed down. Rick was really a good boyfriend; he was just under a lot of pressure.

After the dust settled, Rick seemed to stop coming home every night, and when he did, he barely talked to me. One night, all of a sudden, he told me that I needed to get a place of my own. My belly had just started growing, so I knew Rick had been serious when he told me that I was going to have to deal with it, not him. I was so scared. I hadn't ever lived alone before. I didn't make much money working shifts at The Family Diner, but I knew I couldn't argue with Rick; he didn't like it much when I disagreed with him. So the next day when I went to work, I asked Heather, a girl I worked with, how I could go about finding a place I could afford. I wanted to be brave when I was talking to her, seeing how Heather's husband was in the army, and usually out of the country, leaving her home alone with three kids. She was brave, and I didn't want her to think I was a baby myself.

Heather gave me some good advice. She told me about some housing community that I could probably get into and afford. I wanted to know there was a place to go, but I wasn't in a hurry. I had been feeling lots better, but I would be so tired when I got home from work, I would end up sleeping the rest of my time away.

Rick had been out of a job for a few weeks, but he wasn't staying at home. I figured he must have met somebody and was staying with her. I didn't ask because I didn't want to know the truth. But one day Rick came home and said that was it, I needed to go. Even though I didn't want us to break up, I at least had my baby, so I wasn't really going to be alone. I decided I would call that place Heather told me about.

Boy, did things start happening fast. I woke early for work the next morning, cleaned the diner, called the housing office, made a quick stop at home after work, and then went straight to see the place. Seeing how I don't have a car, I walked home after work, and then used what little money I had left to take a cab over to Willow Wick. As soon as I met the lady in the office, Debbie, I knew she was a good lady. I felt comfortable telling her the private information I had to tell her in order to apply for housing. Luckily, I still had my pay stub in my purse; Debbie said that was the only paperwork I needed since I didn't have a driver's license or own anything else. I had to fill out a packet of papers for Debbie because Willow Wick was funded by the government. I needed all the help I could get, but I also told myself that me and my angel-baby wasn't going to live here forever, just for now.

No sooner did I get home than the phone rang. I thought Debbie must be a guardian angel sent from heaven, because she said I qualified for housing, and that I could move in six days from now. I felt happy and sad at the same time. I started to cry; I think all of those baby hormones must have been making me feel so crazy inside.

Rick didn't come home for a couple of days, so I decided to take my time packing up the few things I had. I knew I wasn't bringing much, just some clothes and a box of old things I saved from growing up. I sure didn't want to leave without at least telling Rick good-bye. I knew he still loved me, and that this wouldn't be the end, but still, I wanted to do what he had asked me to do by moving out.

Sitting on the couch one afternoon for about an hour, I started to feel sleepy. I had to close my eyes for just a minute. Well, what I thought would be a minute ended up being two hours. The loud sound of a door slamming woke me up fast. My heart was pounding. Rick was finally home.

"What are you still doing here?" Rick said with a hard voice.

"I was waiting for you to get home before I left. I found a place to live. It's called—"

"I don't care what it's called or where it is. You could live in a dumpster for all I care. You're nothing but trash."

With my head hung low, I fought back my tears and pretended Rick wasn't talking to me. How I let him make me feel so bad, I don't know. Even though he could be so mean, he had loved me like nobody else. He took care of me for nearly two whole years, and I felt like I owed him so much. It's weird: Rick had treated me better than anybody else had, but he had also treated me the worst.

He walked back into the bedroom; I could hear the shower running. I called the same cab company I had used the week before when I got a ride to Willow Wick the first time. I slowly made my way to the door so I could wait for my ride outside.

I haven't been here that long. And Rick has visited me lots of times. Sometimes it's good; sometimes it's not. I usually keep to myself, except with Gladys. She has saved me from going crazy all by myself. She's my neighbor, and she doesn't like Rick, but she loves me and my angel-baby. I call her G. We do favors for each other because we're friends. Well, maybe not friends because of our age difference, but she looks after me like a granddaughter, and I look to her as a nice kind of granny. G brings me homemade soul food that tastes just like heaven. And I've put drapes together for G. She says God gave me the gift to sew.

Chapter 5

Looking for my car keys, I yelled upstairs that we needed to leave. The children ran down the stairs and, as I reached for my keys, Justin handed me my purse, too. I thanked him, gave him a quick squeeze, and told him that I loved him. The three of us walked out of the house on our way to a late lunch. I wanted to try a new place; it looked like a hole-in-the-wall, but I had heard the food and service was phenomenal. Rachael was not one for trying new things, but I didn't think it was going to hurt her to try. Plus, I thought it would be nice to have a restaurant that only the children and I had gone to together.

Looking at the menu, I asked Rachael and Justin if they had given any thought to what they would like for Christmas. Thanksgiving was around the corner, and this was the first year I did not already have my ducks in a row. This had been a unique year for all of us, to say the least. Before Rachael could even get a syllable out, she pointed, with eyes wide, at a stitched purse being carried by a woman passing by. The purse was striking; it looked like an original from some boutique. Recognizing the excited reaction Rachael was having, I quickly called out to the young lady attached to the purse.

"Excuse me! Excuse me, ma'am."

The woman turned around. Our eyes met. To my amazement, it was Leah, the pregnant girl I had recently met. I could not believe that she and I were in the same place at the same time. I thought, what could be the odds of this happening?

"Yes. Did you call me?"

"Wow. Yes. Leah, isn't it? How are you?"

"I'm good," Leah replied, recognition dawning in her eyes.

I think Rachael and Justin could tell there was a hint of awkwardness in the air; they must have known I knew this stranger because I knew her name, but they remained quiet. I began to converse with Leah. "I don't want to intrude, but let me introduce you to my children, Justin and Rachael." I quickly turned to the children and told them Leah and I had met recently. I then focused my attention back on Leah and explained how upon discussing the upcoming holiday, her exquisite purse had caught Rachael's attention. "May I ask where you bought it?"

Laughing, Leah said, "I didn't buy this, I made it."

Blown away by the talent necessary to make such a beautiful accessory, I was speechless. Rachael must have been thinking a mile a minute because the next thing out of her mouth was "Mom, will you pay your friend Leah to make another one for me?"

Embarrassed by Rachael's impulsivity, I immediately reprimanded her for sounding so rude. I apologized to Leah. Yet, to my surprise, Leah seemed genuinely flattered, and answered right back with an astounding, "Yes."

This was all so unexpected, to run into Leah again, but I chalked it up to fate. Leah and I briefly spoke about this business deal Rachael had created within a two-minute encounter. Leah vaguely explained how she worked at the diner, and that she was there to pick up her paycheck. I told her that I would feel more comfortable discussing the purse order in private, especially since the gift was for Rachael. I asked Leah how I could contact her. She asked if I could stop by the diner on Monday or Tuesday to talk with her. I told her it was a plan and that I looked forward to seeing her then. The children and I finished our meal and enjoyed each others' company for the rest of the weekend.

Monday morning came early; they always seem to snap me out of my emotional roller coasters and back into the reality of routine. The kids were up and ready for school as I began heading off to the office. I had worked for the same advertising agency for sixteen years. Before the children were born, I was quickly moving up the ladder and landing big accounts. I helped organize departments, hire workers, and get the business started from ground zero. Once my children were born, Daniel finished law school and began his own firm, and I had the luxury of deciding to either quit altogether or keep my foot in the door and continue to work as a part-time, contracted advertiser. I was so thankful to have gone with my gut instinct and continued my work, even if my involvement was now somewhat limited. I had felt then that giving up on my career altogether would somehow be the same as giving up an interesting, intriguing part of me that had nothing to do with Daniel or the children. They were my life at the time, but part of my old life would remain intact as long as I kept my career.

With the divorce finalized and my children reaching an age of semi-independence, I thought that now was the perfect time to ask Jack Rankquish, my boss, to hire me back full-time. I respected that he had allowed me to continue with the company all these years as a part-time employee. I worried that he wouldn't want to give me back some of the bigger accounts, since I had put this job on the back burner for the past eleven years.

I was very excited and anxious to meet with Jack that morning. Our meeting was at 8:00, but I took some extra time to make myself look professional: hair up, stylish but sober suit, and not too much makeup. After all, I was one woman in a department of twelve men, some of whom I had hired myself years ago. My mother was not too keen on the idea of my meeting with Jack this morning. She said to me on the phone, "Now, Drew, this is not the time to set yourself up for any kind of rejection. If it were not to work out the way you hope, I fear you would fall right back to where you were before, emotionally, and you have come so far with your depression and all."

This made me all the more determined to get myself back in the game. "Now is the time," I insisted. "I can't sit around any longer, dwelling on the past. I'm trying to move forward." I could tell by her silence that I had not reassured her by any means.

As I walked toward the enormous brick building, I felt so small and insignificant. Once I was inside, however, it gave off the opposite feeling, one of home. That was what I had always loved about the old building. Even the decor made me feel powerful. The floors were gleaming hardwood, and the furniture looked a bit like something you would find in an old, English-style mansion. There were autographed pictures of celebrities along the walls, all of whom had worked with our agency and kept in close touch with Mr. Rankquish himself. He was now a very wealthy, ambitious man, famous in his own right. Working for him had also helped Daniel when he was starting his firm. He would come to all my work parties and hand out business cards. I remembered feeling so proud to be by his side. Now I realized that, in many ways, he had been at my side, using me as a stepping stone. He hadn't gone to my work functions because he was proud of me and what I was accomplishing; he'd gone to gain clients for his own pursuit of happiness. How could I have been so blind to all his selfishness?

My thoughts were interrupted by Jack's secretary telling me to go inside. As I stepped into his office, I noticed two men I didn't recognize sitting alongside Jack. "Ah, Drew, so good to see you. How are the kids?" Jack asked as I sat down on the other side of a conference table roughly the size of a football field.

"They are just wonderful, Jack, thank you for asking," I said, trying to sound as friendly as possible.

"What brings you here today to meet with me, Drew? Is everything okay?" he inquired kindly but in a way that left me feeling slightly intimidated nonetheless.

"Yes, everything's fine. But before we get started, would you mind introducing me to your friends here?" I really wanted some privacy, but I wanted to find a polite way to go about getting it.

"Oh, my apologies, on my right is Dan Goldstein, Richard's son, and on my left, my future son-in-law, Graham Peterson. They're my new partners. Any decisions to be made will be made in consultation with them," he said, giving me a meaningful look. "I thought that bringing fresh new ideas from these brilliant young minds would be the boost our company needs to, you know, take it to the next level."

Hearing Jack say this made me very sad. I remembered when we first began the agency, how Jack always took pride in the fact that he ran the company in a welcoming fashion, with family values. We would all be able to talk to one another and make group decisions. And now I was talking to three men, two of whom had no idea who I was or what my history with the company was, and my professional future lay in their hands. Why should they have the authority to determine what was best for me? How could they even pretend to know?

I decided to proceed with my conversation and to ignore my reservations for the moment. Surely Jack would still help wherever he could. "Well, Jack, I've decided to return to work full-time. My children are growing up, and I am ready to be dedicated to the agency on a full-time basis again. As you recall, I was once your top agent, and I know I will be better than ever."

Before Jack could answer my request, one of the new young suits spoke up and said, "Well, Mrs. Warren, we would love to have you putting in more hours at the agency. However, several changes have taken place since you were here full-time. We understand that you had a big part in the birth of this company. However, in order for us to welcome you back full-time, you are going to have to prove yourself. And using our evaluation system, over time, you do have the potential to increase your salary, just as our current, committed full-time employees have done."

"So," I said with a bit of tartness in my tone, "you are saying that in order for me to increase my hours, my clients, and my salary, I would have to find away to impress you, even though I have been working here for over sixteen years?"

They all began shifting in their chairs and avoiding eye contact. Suddenly, the other young man decided to chime in. "We feel that if this is important to you, it is important to us, and we would like to offer you a two-year time period in which your hours and salary would go up in increments every four months. At the end of the two years, we will evaluate your status and see how well you have proven yourself, and then we can discuss offering you a permanent, full-time position."

Was he serious? What in the hell was I hearing? I knew for sure there were brand-new faces coming in all the time, fresh out of college, who started out with forty hours a week and an awesome salary. These were people with no experience other than their degrees. Then it dawned on me that all of those new faces had been men's.

Disgusted, I stood up and looked Jack in the eyes and said, "Well, gentlemen, I will have to think about this." Jack tried to smile understandingly but said nothing as I walked out the door.

I held my breath until I got to my car, and then I let it all out. I sat in the front seat, holding my face in my hands, and I sobbed. What had happened to Jack? Why did it seem as though everyone around me was changing? This was so unlike Jack. How could he turn his back on me like this? As I put the key in the ignition and began to drive away, all I could say to myself was, "Okay, Mom, you were right."

I began to think about where I had to go now. I needed someone to talk to, a shoulder to cry on. That is when I realized for the first time how alone I was. The kids were in school, the people I once thought were my friends were now excluding me and gossiping about me and my children, and my parents live in Virginia. Calling them while I was upset only hurt them worse, because they were too far away to do anything to help. I couldn't call Kelly, my best friend, because taking a phone call while on duty as a neonatal nurse was against protocol; I would just have to wait.

In the past, I would have gone home to Daniel. Even though he was very self-absorbed, he always made me feel better by giving some arrogant response like, "Screw them, Drew! Are you going to let some self-centered stiff bring you down, or are you going to stand strong like we Warrens know how to do?"

He'd had a way of infusing me with his confidence back then. A part of me wanted to call him and tell him what had happened. After all, he had watched me grow with the company. He knew Jack and the others. He might be able to help me come to a decision. I began to dial his number on my cell phone. I got his voice mail. Listening to his voice on the message was so comforting to me, just what I needed to hear. When I heard the tone to leave my name and number, I suddenly felt nervous. "Hi, Daniel, it's me…um…Drew. Listen, I wanted to ask you about something, so if you could please call me back, I would really like to talk with you." I hung up the phone and hoped that he would call me right back. But he didn't.

As I began to travel toward home, I passed Pepe's Pizza Parlor, Daniel's favorite place to eat. I could remember at least a hundred times I'd picked up pizza to eat at home while snuggling up with Daniel on a family night. I missed those days. I suddenly realized I hadn't eaten all morning, so I thought I'd take advantage of my location. It was early, but luckily Pepe's opened at 10:00 a.m, so I wouldn't have to wait long. After all, I really had no place to go, no deadlines to meet. As soon as the red, neon "open for business" light began glowing, I found a small booth in the corner and waited for the waitress.

I looked out the restaurant window and saw a familiar sight: a shiny black Jaguar. Was it Daniel? What fate that would be to see him stopping in for a bite. I would love to talk with him face-to-face, like the good old days. I looked out the restaurant window anxiously as the car door opened, but it was Julie who stepped out. She was driving my car. The same car I used to come to Pepe's in, time after time, to pick up Daniel's favorite pepperoni and extra cheese pizza for him and the kids. My stomach sank into my knees, and I quickly hid behind the menu. I listened as the owner's son, Tony, came to the register.

"Hey, Julie," he said with a smile.

"Hey, Tony! Pizza ready?" she asked.

"You bet," he replied as he handed her the box and said sarcastically, "Hold the pepperoni, right?"

They both laughed, and I almost broke down in tears as I heard Julie say, "Oh please, you know how much Daniel loves your pepperoni pizza. I'm going to get fat from eating your pizzas all the time." She paid Tony and left with a smile. I watched as she gently opened the car's passenger-side door and placed the pizza securely in the front seat next to the driver's side, just as I had done for years.

As she drove off, the waitress came over to me and asked for my order. "Thank you," I said. "But I'm not hungry anymore."

I got up and left, hoping neither Tony nor any other familiar face would recognize mine. How embarrassing. People who once knew me, my husband, and my children, now knew Julie. I had been replaced. My sorrow began to turn to anger as I got in the car and started the engine. How could he bring Julie to our special place? How could Julie stand to drive that car, knowing it was once mine? Did she not have any self-respect? Couldn't she demand her own car? Her own special restaurant? Was she purposely trying to live my life instead of making a life of her own? I then thought about the vacation Daniel wanted to take during the week of my birthday. My anger bubbled over, thinking about him planning that trip. Did Julie know it was my birthday, and was she trying to sabotage me by taking my children away during that meaningful time?

My cell phone rang, making me jump. It was Daniel, returning my message. I was now so happy he hadn't answered before. I didn't need advice from him. What was I thinking? He was the problem. I could find my own way.

I answered the call and Daniel said, "Drew—what do you need to talk about? I'm really busy." Busy waiting for your princess to bring your pizza, I thought to myself.

"Yes, Daniel, I'm so happy you called me back. About your ski trip in February, yeah, it's a no-go."

"What the hell are you talking about, Drew?" he asked. I could picture him, face turning red, veins popping out on his forehead. The thought of it actually gave me a pleasant feeling.

"Well, it turns out my mom is having us all up to Virginia to celebrate my birthday that week, so the kids will not be going with you." I said it with such vigor and confidence I totally surprised myself.

"Drew," he said in a much calmer voice. It was that same manipulating tone he used on his clients to suck them into his plotting and scheming. "I told you we already have reservations, and the kids are excited about it. You're not going to let them down, are you?" he asked.

"Well, actually," I said in a very upbeat, excited voice, "I believe you already let them down when you decided to walk out of our house and leave them behind. So my saying no to this one little vacation will never compare to the years of pain and anguish you have and will cause them. They're not going. You and Julie will have to enjoy the slopes on your own. Have a good day, Daniel."

I hung up the phone and paused for about thirty seconds, pondering what had just happened. Then I began to laugh. I laughed so hard I had to pull over. People walking on the sidewalk next to my car saw me and smiled at the crazy woman who continued to laugh hysterically for about three minutes. I realized that I had not laughed that hard in years. Damn, it felt good. A day that was once full of disappointment and embarrassment was looking up after all. I had no idea where the spurt of confidence was coming from. Perhaps insanity and despair, perhaps hitting rock bottom. Wherever or whatever the source, it didn't matter. I liked it. I loved myself this way. Maybe this was the new beginning everyone kept telling me about. I seemed to get it now.

Chapter 6

Thanksgiving is a time when families remember times past, share laughter, and hope for the future. This year our holiday was anything but traditional; my children were going to leave me at 6:00 p.m. to wake up on Thanksgiving morning at Daniel's house. I came to the realization, early on, that there was nothing glorious about physical-custodial holidays, and the compassion expressed between the lines on divorce decrees was nonexistent. It was only five o'clock in the morning; I lied in bed feeling lethargic. I knew that once I got up I would have to start the day, and from that point forward, it was just a matter of time until the children would be gone. Living in denial was impossible. I fought back the tears once Rachael and Justin were awake. I did not want to make them feel guilty for leaving me, or make them regret staying because they felt sorry for me, so I made the decision to take a positive approach to our precious time. Since we had the whole day open, I suggested the three of us take a ride to Helen, a small German-themed town outside of Cleveland, Georgia. We loved to walk around the town, indulge in some homemade fudge and delicious pralines, and on this particular day, we also had the pleasure of watching hot air balloons lift off into the sky. Helen was only about an hour away from home, yet it made you feel like you were in another world. I was thoroughly enjoying our day trip, but I knew we were on the clock and had to head back soon.

Arriving home with forty-five minutes to spare, the children and I relaxed on the couch, with the television turned off, and laughed as we retold old stories. Times like these made me realize how grateful I really was, and how truly blessed. The time escaped me; the next thing I knew, the doorbell rang.

Rachael sprang to the door to greet her father. My heart sank—I couldn't help it. I watched the children as they got into car, with decorative Julie sitting shotgun; I stood at the door with a perma-grin across my face, waving as they pulled out of the driveway. I could not help but wonder why Daniel was always so happy. Was he faking contentment? I mean, seriously, how could he be so happy? In all honesty, Rachael and Justin were with me the majority of the time, and knowing how broken I was on the inside about the concept of sharing my children, I thought Daniel should be even more torn up than me, because he didn't get to spend nearly as much time with them. My level of frustration was reaching a maximum because I found myself pondering why Daniel would say the things he did, or why he would behave the way he did. I admit, I spent too much time attempting to figure out the underlying reasons for responses or even ideas Daniel expressed. Many times, I discovered that I was really just beating myself up over the smallest things; I was my own punching bag. I eventually found myself getting mad, exuding negative energy that was ultimately irrelevant.

I closed the door once I could not see Daniel's car any longer. What was I going to do for Thanksgiving? I had already promised myself that I would refuse any invitation to spend this family holiday with some other family, and not my own. And I was a woman of my word. Kelly, of course, had invited me over, but I acted brave and declined. My parents were too far away to join them for a dessert plate of my mother's famous homemade pecan pie. I felt like I needed a good cry, and then a big dose of reality.

I knew that if I could make it through the night without the children, 8:00 p.m. the next evening would come sooner than later. It was probably about 7:00 on the eve of Thanksgiving, when I decided to pick up something for dinner. Nothing beats eating Chinese in bed while watching some comedy that required no brainpower to understand.

Making my way towards The Buddha House, I felt a weight lifted from my chest. I don't know how or why this feeling came over me, but it did. Wishing I had had a menu at home, so I could have ordered in advance and then done a quick pickup, I figured I'd just pretend I wasn't bothered by the fact that I was waiting for my dinner-for-one. No sooner did I walk in than my attention was summoned.

"Hey. Hey, I know you," said a somewhat familiar voice.

Identifying the voice was difficult, until my eyes rested on the young pregnant girl I had recently befriended. Sometimes it is hard to put a name with a face when the encounter is in a different environment than the one you originally knew the person from. But in this case, Leah was no chameleon. Of course the fact that she was pregnant was the first identifier. Leah had frequently crossed my mind, leaving a strong impression.

I replied, "Yes, Leah, how are you?

"Good. You picking up dinner for you and your kids?"

"No. Actually, Rachael and Justin are with their father this evening."

I immediately asked Leah if she had eaten, and she replied that she had not. Without a second thought, I invited her to join me for dinner.

I found myself in a vulnerable state of mind. I began to shed some light on my own life by confiding in Leah. Although we led different lives, I needed a sympathetic ear to listen to my tale on what I found to be a sad evening.

Unraveling my story of divorce, leaving out some painful details, I found myself telling Leah that I was a woman with a broken heart. During our conversation, I told her my heart had been broken by Daniel, but more so because of the consequences of the divorce. Clearly, I was crushed by the fact that I had to share my precious children whom I loved with all of my heart. Being separated from them on holidays and every other weekend was hard for me to accept. This was not something I was not prepared for or ever thought would happen to me.

"You are a great mother." Leah said confidently. "Although you can't be with your kids all of the time, you at least make the most of the time you are together. The three of you looked so happy that time I saw you at the diner. Even after I left you that day, I thought how lucky you were to have such a perfect family. I can't wait to have that kind of relationship with my angel baby." Rubbing her stomach as we spoke, Leah beamed with a maternal glow.

As we enjoyed Singapore noodles and mixed veggies, the conversation became lighter, and we began to laugh like two old friends. The evening was refreshing, and my mood was lifted. I did not want to be a bitter woman; I owed it to Leah for making me a better person that night. I figured I was going to sulk and cry the night away, but instead I had shared a meal with somebody who opened my eyes to an optimistic view of life. There are not many people in this world like Leah, who somehow seem to find the silver lining in tough situations. Considering the hand she had been dealt in life, her positive energy was inspiring.

Chapter 7

I used to watch movies late at night about families and what their holidays were really like. I loved watching The Christmas Story with the little boy named Ralphie. I was always jealous of all the parts with the family eating together every night and shopping for a Christmas tree. I did try and make the holidays special in my own way. I would sew gifts for all the teachers at school and people in our neighborhood. It was fun for me, and they really seemed to love what I came up with. Every year, people would come by from the local churches to bring Granny and me gifts on Christmas Eve. I guess they knew we were poor and they wanted to help. My favorite part was watching the looks on their faces as I would open up the box with a new doll or a pretty new sweater. It made me happy knowing that they were happy. They would give Granny money to buy food, and she always bought us a turkey. We would even have some of Granny's friends from her cards group over on Christmas Eve. They would bring me gifts, too. I felt so thankful to get anything, but I never had that experience of telling someone what I really wanted and then hoping and hoping I would get it, like Ralphie did with his Red Ryder BB

Gun in that movie. I would just get surprises that people thought a poor little girl like me would want. The funny thing is, I would take the clothes off the new dolls and cut up my new sweaters and shirts to sew gifts for other people. I never really felt poor because I got a lot of hand-me-down clothes donated from church, and they were actually very nice clothes. Maybe not as expensive as some other kids' at school, but they were clean and up-to-date.

Granny also made money cutting and styling hair in our house. It was all "under the table," she would say. I think that means she would just put it in her pocket and not pay taxes on it. Granny also got money for taking care of me since Mama died. Granny said she used that money to buy us food and pay the bills. Melissa, a neighbor girl I played with, told me that her mama said that money was really mine for college or the future, and that Granny shouldn't spend it like that. I didn't know what to believe. I was just happy I had food in the house when I needed some. Granny kept busy during the holidays, doing all her old lady friends' hair, as well as people around the neighborhood. She would also keep my hair trimmed and nice, not because she loved me, but because she said it was good for her business.

"I can't be having you run around looking like a rag doll if I'm trying to get people's business," she would tell me as I sat in her styling chair in the kitchen while she washed, trimmed, and brushed my blond hair. She would always have it looking shiny for the people who would come over after church. I think now she was just trying to make it look like she was the best granny in the world. Really I think that she just wanted to keep caring for me as long as she got those checks coming in each month. Ever since Granny died and her house was rented out by a relative of hers, I always wondered what happened to those checks. Did they just stop? It seems like I could have gone and talked with some people about it, but then I was always afraid they would make me live in a foster home or something, so I just kept quiet and let Rick handle everything.

Just thinking about the holidays of the past gave me a weird feeling. It was a sad time for me, and now things were so different. I had the chance to turn it all around. I didn't have to pretend to be happy anymore. I could act whatever way I wanted to act and feel whatever I wanted to feel. It was so great to spend Thanksgiving with Drew. When we were sitting at the table in the Chinese restaurant, I would watch people walk by and look at us and smile. I bet they thought Drew was my mama and we were out for some lunch together. Mother and daughter. I pretended this was true while we were sitting there. I would look at Drew when she was talking to me, and I noticed how truly beautiful she was. Her hair and skin were so perfect. I wish I had a mother just like her. I really hope I get to see her again because, for whatever reason, she makes me feel important, just like Mrs. Baker did. Drew listens to me and likes to hear my stories. I'd like to tell her my whole story someday. About my mama dying when I was in middle school and about the times when Granny would tell me bad stories about my daddy and how I never had any real connection to who I was. Or would all these things scare Drew away? Maybe she has never met anyone as messed up as me. Maybe she wouldn't want to hear those kinds of stories.

Today I am getting out for a bit, and I need to start getting ready. I am going to ask Gladys to drop me off at the mall to shop around a little. I got some extra money from the owners at the diner for a Christmas bonus, and I thought I could get a couple of things for the baby and something for Rick.

I went over to ask Gladys for a ride, and she said she would drop me off while she went to the post office. This late November day was one of those kinds of days that remind you that Christmas is coming soon. It was cool and damp, no leaves on the trees. The sky was gray with swirls of dark blue clouds.

"I sure wish that I could paint, Gladys," I told her while we were in the car together. "This sky would make a pretty picture for sure."

Gladys laughed and replied, "Only you could look at the gray, dreary sky and make something beautiful out of it, Leah."

"Well, I love looking at the sky. It looks different every day. Everything else around me seems to stay the same. But if I want something different to look at, I can just look up."

"I think you should be a preacher, Leah. You know how to make everything and everybody seem better," Gladys said kindly.

"Did I tell you that I ran into that nice lady who brought me the baby clothes again?" I asked Gladys.

"No, you sure didn't. How was it? She seems like such a nice lady."

"She is so nice. We were both eating Chinese food for Thanksgiving. She was sad that her kids were gone, and I was sad that Rick didn't come over, so we kept each other company. Turns out she lives just around the way, so we go to a lot of the same places. I'm really getting to like her. She's so sweet," I said as I replayed a bit of that day again in my mind.

"I'm happy you have someone else who seems to be looking out for you, Leah. As old as I'm getting, I don't know how much longer I'll be around to see that you are taken care of," Gladys said with a giggle.

"G, don't go talking like that. You're going to be around here for a long time to come."

"I guess you're right, Leah," Gladys said as she rode up to the front of the mall entrance. "Now, I'll meet you back here at three o'clock. Don't keep me waiting."

"Yes, ma'am. I'll be here," I reassured her. "Thank you, Gladys."

As I entered the mall, I noticed all of the beautiful Christmas decorations hanging from the ceilings of every store. The music was playing all of the familiar Christmas carols, and people were dressed up in their holiday colors. I usually don't like going to the mall much. I can never really afford to buy anything here. But I was feeling good and wanted to experience the "hustle and bustle" everyone is always complaining about at work.

"Oh, don't go to the mall," they would say, "It is crazy there now."

Well, call me crazy, but I love it. I love to see people rushing around with bags in their arms and dragging their kids kicking and screaming. I wonder if that will be me one day with my baby. I hope I'll be busy trying to find things to put under the tree, and I dream about having that look on my face. The look of exhaustion from trying to pick the right gift. This was going to be a fun day for me. A day to see how the "real world" acts.

I decided to step into the baby store to look at baby clothes. I really didn't need much after all the gifts from Drew, but I thought it would be fun to look. There were lots of pregnant women in the store, all much older than me, grabbing things off the rack as if they were going to disappear. I started listening to some of their conversations.

"Oh, look at this one. The material is so soft."

"Yes, but those snaps may pinch the baby. Get the zipper instead."

"I don't like that fabric, it's too scratchy."

This kind of talk went on and on. I was amazed that these women took that much time to argue about clothes for a baby who doesn't even care about those things yet. It seemed really silly to me. I decided to get out of that store and head down to the Gap to find Rick a new shirt for Christmas. I wondered if he cared if it was scratchy or if it had zippers. Just as I was picking up a few things, I heard a familiar voice behind me.

"Leah! How's it going, girl?"

Before I knew it, I was being embraced by a gorgeous, bulky, red-headed, sweet-smelling guy. It was Robbie, and he was no longer just the boy who sat in front of me in math class. He was now this muscular, clean-shaven guy. I must have stared at him for what seemed like two minutes before he said, "Well, aren't you going to even say hi to me? You know, 'nice to see you' or something?"

I finally gathered my wits about myself and answered a bit pathetically. "Robbie, you have grown," I said, immediately thinking that was so stupid.

"Well, you know, I play college ball for Boston so they really keep me buff. I get hit by some pretty tough guys now. Not like high school anymore. So what have you been up to?"

I immediately thought about the baby. I realized I wasn't showing much as of yet, so it probably looked like I'd just gained a few pounds. I really didn't think it was anything I needed to tell him right here, in the middle of the Gap.

"Well, I'm working, and I have my own place," I told him with a smile. I was happy I didn't have to lie to him.

"Wow, that's great, Leah. It is really good to see you," he said, staring at me intently. He was quiet for a moment, and then he said, "Hey, maybe before I go back, we can catch up on a few things. I think Brian is having a New Year's party. Maybe you can come to that," Robbie said excitedly.

"Maybe," I told him reluctantly. "I'll try."

"Okay. If you need a ride, just let me know. Look me up in the phone book. You can leave a message with my parents. Well, I gotta run, I'll see you at the party, okay?" he said as he turned and walked away.

I waved good-bye as I watched him rejoin a bunch of his buddies who were waiting outside of the store. I couldn't believe what had just happened. I couldn't believe that Robbie just asked me to a party. I wished I had someone to call and share this with. But there was no one. Gladys would listen, but she really isn't the one to share this kind of news with. If only I had Drew's number. I bet she would really like to hear that story. The sad part of it all is I knew I would not call Robbie. I would not go to the New Year's party. Rick would probably have plans for us that night. Besides, I was having a baby, and I couldn't pretend that I wasn't. I couldn't do what all the other kids my age were doing. I was going to be a mother. I had to find a place to sit for a minute and gather my thoughts. I felt weak in the knees after seeing Robbie and how handsome he was. He and I were now further apart than ever. He could never know what was really going on with me. I wanted him to just always think that I was fine. I wanted him to always think that it is truly good to see me, just like he said. I don't want him to be disappointed. I knew I'd definitely start watching his games on TV, and I would probably be dreaming about being his girlfriend and being at home, waiting for him to return after a long game. Those would be good dreams.

I finished up my shopping and grabbed a bite to eat. As I was sitting down in the fast food restaurant, a young mother came in pushing her baby girl in her stroller. They both looked very happy, and the baby was making those cute little baby noises and kicking her feet. I felt a sense of peace inside. I may never have Robbie, but I'd have my baby, and that would be worth all the heartache and sacrifices I have made over my eighteen years of living. It would all make sense then. Christmas is coming, and surely Rick would get more and more excited about the baby as time drew closer. Maybe we could even go and pick out a tree together or something. I laughed to picture Rick picking out a tree. He would probably want to get it home and decorate it with old beer bottle caps or something. With that thought, I hurried outside to meet Gladys. It was about time for her to be here, and I had gotten everything I needed. I decided not to tell her or anyone else about my running into Robbie. I would just keep that a little secret. Sometimes it's nice to hold things inside for only you to enjoy. This was a good day, and I just needed to leave it at that.

Chapter 8

It was the day before Christmas Eve, and I was feeling a bit more at ease about my situation. This morning I even found myself humming along with the radio as I began baking sugar cookies in the kitchen. Perhaps it was the "spirit in the air" or the way my children hold those excited looks on their faces when they pass the Christmas tree. I began to think of Christmases of the past, but this time I didn't feel as much heartache as I thought I would. I knew my children would be with me, and my parents would be arriving today for a visit as well. It was going to be a very nice time even though Daniel would not be a part of it. I had even asked Leah during our meeting at the diner if I could take her with us to church on Christmas Eve. Leah agreed, but said she would feel more comfortable meeting us there. I was actually relieved about that, as my car was going to be very full with all of us. My friend Kelly is also joining us for church with her family. It should be a wonderful day to share. It is always a beautiful sermon. We light candles and sing "Silent Night" around the cross, and it is a true reminder of the suffering of others. Nothing in life is easy, and I am really beginning to let that all sink in.

Noon came quickly, and the doorbell rang. The kids came tearing down the steps to race to the door to greet Pop and Grams. They threw the door open, and there were yells of greeting and laughter and hugs as my parents were nearly knocked over at the door. It took us about twenty minutes to unload gift after gift from all parts of the car.

"Mom, Dad, you shouldn't have," I said, just as I do every year.

"We know," Mom replied. "We just don't get to see the kids as often as we like, so we give it all we've got when we do."

We didn't even stop to take a breath before Mom and Dad were up in the bedrooms looking at all the kids' awards, trophies, and artwork. I was trying to arrange the mounds of gifts under the tree in some type of orderly fashion. The truth is that I get just as excited as the kids do seeing all of the gifts under the tree. I just know how to contain myself.

I finished getting dinner ready and tried to settle the kids in with a movie. We made it an early night, seeing as the next day was Christmas Eve and we would probably be up really late. I went to bed feeling happy for the first time in a long while. I was feeling stronger and more confident. I thought that the holidays would really set me back, but getting through Thanksgiving without having a total nervous breakdown was a confidence-builder for me. I realized that having that time with Leah also really did replace an empty part of me on that day. I was excited to see her tomorrow for church and hoped that she would really come. I was hoping she was excited as well.

Christmas Eve was a day of leisure. We watched old movies like *It's a Wonderful Life* and *A Christmas Story*, the kids' favorite. My dad is the type who enjoys the Chevy Chase version of the holidays, *National Lampoon's Christmas Vacation*. We sat around the living room floor with the fire going, eating sugar cookies and fudge. It was just wonderful. I did have moments of sadness throughout the day, thinking about Daniel and what he and Julie might be up to. Were they doing the same thing, only with her family or were they home alone together? Was he thinking about me or the kids at all? I would then quickly snap myself out of these thoughts and try to concentrate on the now and being with the people I love.

Before you knew it, it was time to head out to church. I told Kelly to get there a bit early to save us all a spot in the pew. I described Leah to Kelly and asked her to keep an eye out for her. As we drove over to church, I filled my parents in on the details of my encounters with Leah. They were both very quiet for a while. I think they weren't sure what to expect when I told them we were taking a pregnant eighteen-year-old girl to church. My mother finally spoke out.

"Drew, you were always the type of girl who wanted to make everybody happy. Sounds to me like you are a great role model for this young girl."

"Yeah," Rachael piped in from the back seat, "And she makes these awesome purses!"

"She does, Mom," I added. "She's very talented."

"Well, we look forward to meeting her," my dad said.

As we got to church, we saw that it was very crowded. We saw Kelly standing up and waving towards the front, and we headed that way. I passed many friends who smiled with concern, knowing that Daniel was not here with me. In reality, there were many times I brought the children to church without him. He always said he worked so hard during the week that he needed his weekends to rest. It didn't bother me at the time. But now that I look back, those were just more times that we should have shared as a family. I wonder if Daniel would have kept our family together had he been a man of faith. It's something I will never know.

"Hey, Kelly," I said as we approached. I reached over and gave her and her kids a big hug. We all scooted around, taking off our coats and trying to adjust when all of a sudden I looked up and saw Leah standing at the front of the church. She looked just precious in a red, velvet skirt and white top, holding a small, wrinkled, old Bible in one hand and a gift bag in the other. Her eyes were scanning the crowd, looking for us.

"Leah, over here!" I said, waving my arms to get her attention. Leah came over, and I introduced her to my parents and then to Kelly and her children.

"You remember Justin and Rachael?" I asked, pointing in their direction.

"Why sure I do. I even have a little something for them."

Leah reached into her gift bag and pulled out two small, handmade gifts. One was a pink purse with beautiful jewels all over it for Rachael. The other was a red-and-blue stocking with an Atlanta Braves baseball team logo for Justin.

"Wow, thanks!" Justin and Rachael exclaimed at the same time, moving over to make a space for her right in between them.

"Leah, thank you from the bottom of my heart," I told her as I leaned over and touched her arm. My mother just oohed and aahed over Leah's gifts. It was wonderful.

As the ceremony began, I watched Leah as she listened to every word intently. Her eyes were transfixed on the pastor, and she nodded every now and then. When the lights were dimmed and the candles were lit, we began to sing "Silent Night." Leah went to the front of the church with all of us to light her candle. When she turned around, she saw Robbie Curtis, sitting in the pew just a few rows back with his family. He looked happy and comforted with his parents on either side of him. He didn't notice Leah, and for some reason, she sat down quickly. She looked embarrassed; perhaps she felt uncomfortable being here with someone else's family and not her own. Maybe she didn't want him to know that she was having a baby. Leah suddenly began to behave self-consciously, and then she began to weep silently to herself.

Just then, Rachael leaned over to me and said "Mom, I think Leah is crying." I handed Kelly my candle and whispered to her that I would be back in just a minute. I stood up and beckoned for Leah to come with me out the side door. Leah looked relieved. We went out the side door to a little room where lots of meetings and classes were held during the week. I took Leah in and closed the door.

"Are you okay?" I asked.

Leah began to really cry at this point. "I'm so sorry I'm ruining your Christmas with your family. I can just stay here until my ride comes. You go back in with them," Leah told me.

"No, no, Leah, it's fine. Trust me, I've done my share of crying lately. It's not bothering me a bit, I promise. But, you know, sometimes it helps to have someone to talk to."

Leah sat quietly for a moment and then began to explain a little at a time. "It's just that sometimes I have a hard time around Christmas. I don't know who I'm supposed to be celebrating with. I don't really have a true family. I asked Rick to come, and he told me he would never go to church. He thinks it's a waste of time. Now it got me thinking that I don't want to raise a baby with that kind of person, but I'm stuck. There is no chance for me to be with someone else now. I'm having his baby, and he's going to be in my life forever. He said he won't even marry me because I want to be married in a church, and he thinks that's stupid. The church people were really kind to me when I was young. Christmas presents, clothes, and even food. One of the ladies even brought me this Bible when I was a little girl. I would read parts of it here and there. I kept it with me all this time. Here, look inside."

Leah handed me the Bible, and I opened it up. There was a small inscription on the inside that said, "To Leah,

May the path you choose in life lead you to follow Him.

With love,

Pastor Mosely"

I handed the Bible back to Leah with a sigh. "Leah, I'm sure you have a lot of things you could tell me when you're ready, and I will be here to listen. Right now, you need to do what is right for you and your baby. If Rick is not going to help you and your baby to become better people, then he doesn't need to be in your life. I know what it's like to be afraid to be alone. It's a horrible feeling. But we have to remember that, like the pastor said, we have choices. We all choose a path to take in life. There's the easy road and the hard road, and from what I have always heard, the best road is always the hardest to take."

Saying these things to Leah was very eye-opening for me. What path was I going to choose? One where Daniel dominated my every thought and my sense of self-worth? Or would I choose the harder path, one where I get to reinvent myself? The path I intend to follow is the one I was trying to encourage Leah to follow, too. It's what's right for me and for my children. We cannot be with someone just because we are afraid to be alone. Leah and I seem to both be wrestling with this notion.

Leah and I hugged. We went outside another door and met everyone who was coming out of the service. Leah saw Gladys standing by her car and waved to her. Then, turning to me and to my children, she said, "Well, thank you so much for letting me come to church with all of you. I think I learned a lot."

Rachael hugged Leah and rubbed her soft dress. "I love this dress," she said. "Did you make it?"

"Why, yes, I did, Rachael-girl. I'm glad you like it. The truth is, I make most of my clothes. It keeps me busy."

"Leah," I said as she began to walk off. "I want to come and give you a ride to your next doctor's appointment. I mean, in case Rick forgets. Or maybe I can go with both of you or something. I have a feeling you might need a friend there with you."

"I would like that," Leah said. "It's the Tuesday after Christmas, at two o'clock."

"I'll be there," I said as Leah waved good-bye, got into Gladys's car, and drove off.

At home that evening, after Mom and I put the kids to bed, we stayed up and drank a glass of wine together.

"Church was great, Drew," Mom said. "You have very nice friends."

"Thanks, Mom. I'm so happy you and Dad are here. It will make this the best Christmas yet."

I went to bed anticipating the fun of opening all of our gifts tomorrow and spending the day until Daniel came to get the kids. I am even feeling a bit at peace with the fact that they are leaving. I am choosing a new path. I am beginning to see that there is more to life than my problems. There is a whole world out there with people struggling to find their way. My way is going to be an uphill battle, but I'm getting there. I can confidently say that I will make it.

Chapter 9

On the Tuesday after Christmas, I went to pick up Leah for her doctor's appointment. I pulled into the housing development and tried to remember the exact location of Leah's duplex, but they kind of looked the same. I noticed the sweet lady who was there before and who seemed to watch over Leah. I pulled over to her and asked if she knew where Leah was.

"Oh, yes, honey," she said in a voice that sounded as sweet as honey herself. "She is in that room over there. She's not feeling so well today. Won't seem to come out of the house much. I tried to go there myself but no luck. Leah told me to go away, she don't feel like coming out or letting company in."

I decided to take a chance anyway, and knocked on Leah's door. "Leah, it's me, Drew. It's time for your doctor's appointment," I said nervously. I heard several locks click, and finally the door opened slightly. Leah was pressed up against the door, and she began to speak softly.

"I can't go today. Thanks anyway. I'll talk to you later, okay, Drew?"

I had a bad feeling about the way she was acting and her tone of voice. Call it a motherly instinct, but I knew I needed to see more of her than the barely-open door revealed. "Leah, please open the door. I'm concerned. I want to help you."

As the door opened, it became evident that my intuition was correct. It was bad. One of Leah's eyes was swollen shut, her right cheek was black-and-blue, and her bottom lip was bloody and split wide open.

"Leah!" I gasped. "What happened to you?"

The sweet lady from next door brushed past me into the room. "It was that boyfriend of yours again, wasn't it, sweetie?" she said with a loving voice. It was strange to me to think that she wasn't panicking as much as I was. Was she used to this? Had she seen this so many times before that it didn't startle her as it did me?

"Oh, G, leave it be," Leah said to her. "You know how he gets when he's drinking. He's just under a lot of pressure from work and the baby coming and all."

I could not believe what I was seeing and hearing. If this were my daughter or any of my friends, I would be on the phone to the police to have the man arrested immediately. What were these people thinking?

"Leah, if you know who did this to you, you have to do something! He needs to be arrested for this, do you understand?" I shouted, trying to get a grasp on the situation.

Leah looked at me as if I was from another planet. "Well, if he gets arrested, it would be my fault. How could I live with myself? Besides, I don't have anybody but Rick."

My eyes began to well up with tears. I realized that we were not that different. For many years, I had flown under the radar, letting men take the lead. Daniel controlled the finances and made most of the decisions in the home. He even controlled who our friends were. I have also been controlled by men at work. All of my ideas and new clients were approved by men. Leah was not any different than me. She'd been relying on this man to take her to the doctor when he was good and ready, and now he was physically controlling her, letting her know he was the boss. I would not stand for this. I guess I saw a bit of myself in Leah, except her situation was bigger, darker. It scared me. Right then and there, I made the decision to make a difference. I was not going to turn my back on Leah and her baby. It's been said that if you know better, you do better. I knew better, and I would teach Leah to know better, too. I took Leah by the hands and looked her in the eyes.

"Leah, that may have been true before, but not anymore. You do have somebody—you have me. I will help you. I will not leave you. You can trust me. You have your whole life ahead of you, and you shouldn't live under Rick's thumb or anyone else's. I am not going to watch you struggle, you have my word. We're going to start today. Now, tell me—where is that good-for-nothing excuse for a man?"

Leah hugged me as a small stream of tears fell from her eyes; she thanked me in a soft voice. The next thing I knew, Leah was in the front seat of my car, leading me to some rusty old tavern in town. I've seen this place many times, but I had never in my life dared to enter. As we pulled up, there were only a few beat-up old trucks and a couple of motorcycles outside. After all, it was the middle of the day. It was hard for me to believe that people would start drinking so early and probably continue on throughout the night; it seemed like such a sad life.

I had no idea what we were going to do once we found this Rick character. Something inside me, some driving force had control now. It was like an out of body experience.

"So, Drew. Why do you want to help someone like me anyways?" Leah asked as we parked the car.

I turned to her and looked at her poor beaten face and said, "Well, Leah, in a weird way, we're not so different." We looked at each other for a long moment and then smiled and got out of the car.

"What do you expect me to say when I see him?" Leah asked.

"I want you to tell him that he is not to come in contact with you ever again. Tell him that you don't need anything from him, and if he ever tries to contact you, you'll have him arrested for assault."

"What if I get scared?" Leah asked. She suddenly sounded so young and timid. She had sounded so brave up until now. I realized she was just acting her age.

"That's what I'm here for," I reassured her.

We walked into the bar, and it took a moment to regain my sight. It seemed so dark compared to the outside. There was old seventies-style rock and roll playing on a jukebox in the corner. The bar smelled of stale smoke, probably still lingering from the night before. There were a couple of shady-looking men shooting pool in the back room. I followed Leah, who seemed to know exactly where she was going. There, sitting at the bar, was Rick. He spotted Leah and turned her way. I was surprised to see how old he was. He looked to be at least fifteen years older than Leah. He had tanned skin and greasy, dark hair. He looked as if he had already lived a very rough life. I also noticed when he began to speak how dingy and stained his teeth looked.

"What the hell are you doing here?" he asked Leah. "You didn't come here to ask me for some more money, did you? Well, you ain't getting none, so don't waste your breath."

Leah began to hesitate. I could tell she was not in her element. She seemed to shrink, and her demeanor became childlike: small, insignificant. It was part of an intimidation spell Rick obviously had over her. Rick suddenly turned and noticed me behind Leah.

"Well, well, what have we got here? Leah brought her a friend. Hey, Marty, bring these two fine ladies a beer," Rick said as he turned toward the bartender.

Realizing that this was going nowhere fast, I stepped in front of Leah as her protector and stared right into Rick's eyes. I was still worked up from the shock of seeing Leah's cuts and bruises: the evidence of his abuse. I knew I wasn't going to let this grungy alcoholic back me into a corner.

"I don't know who in the hell you think you are, but you are no longer a part of this girl's life. If you so much as call her on the telephone, I will have your ass thrown in jail so fast you won't even realize what hit you," I bellowed.

"Oh, yeah, lady?" Rick said as he began to stand up in front of his bar stool. "And who exactly might you be?"

"I am Leah's attorney," I lied, "and I am watching your every move. You are already going to be prosecuted for abuse, and from what I hear, you have quite a drug problem as well. How does fifteen years in prison sound to you?" This was not information I knew to be true. It was just another one of those instinctual moments in life we can't always explain. Rick immediately sank back on his bar stool and began to grovel.

"Look, I didn't mean to hurt her. I was drunk and angry," he said as he began to turn toward Leah. "Baby, you know I didn't mean to hurt you, right?" he asked in a whiney, almost tearful, tone of voice.

Leah stepped between Rick and me and began talking in a very nervous, insecure voice. She was speaking to the man she knew as her abuser, as well as her lover. As she began to speak, Rick cut her off, begging for forgiveness again. Leah backed down and stopped speaking. I looked at Rick and firmly asked him to listen to Leah because she had something important to say. He just rolled his bloodshot eyes. I turned back to Leah and suggested she finish what she had started to say. "I can forgive you, Rick. But it's over. Done. I won't let you hurt me again, and I won't let you ever hurt my baby. If you leave us alone, I won't make you pay for anything anymore. I can do it on my own." Then her voice dropped to little more than a whisper as she begged, "Just let me go, Rick, please."

Rick looked a bit saddened but also relieved. Perhaps he knew that he was in no shape to take on any type of responsibility. He was a pathetic, lost soul. I took Leah by the arm and led her outside to the car. Leah was very quiet as we drove to the police station to file a report and to ask for a restraining order against Rick. As Leah spoke with the police, I stood by her side. We were taking baby steps but making progress in getting Leah on her own two feet.

After our business was taken care of at the police station, Leah and I rode back to her home, and I promised to call later to check on her. I encouraged her to call and make another doctor's appointment at the clinic, and I promised I would go with her. Then I gave her a hug and told her I needed to be going. The kids were on their way home. She thanked me and said she had never in her life seen any woman stand up to any man before. She seemed proud, and that made me smile. I knew there was still a lot of work to be done with Leah, but I was committed to helping her. I was also committed to my children, however, and I rushed home to be there in time to see Rachael and Justin get off the bus.

As I made the children a snack, the phone rang. It was Kelly. When she asked, "So what did you do today?" I began to laugh.

"Girl, you need to sit down," I told her. "I have an earful to tell you."

Chapter 10

"Kelly, I am so glad you called. I've had several epiphanies lately, and I want to tell you all about them. You wouldn't believe how I have evolved into a real woman!" I joked.

"I'm so proud of you, Drew. We've been friends since we were twelve years old, and I know you better than anyone. You've always been strong and determined, and I knew it was just a matter of time before you pulled yourself out of this slump. Sometimes we let events in our lives bring us down, but we've never let them defeat us." There was a brief lull in the conversation as I let her words sink in. Then she asked, "Are Rachael and Justin with you tonight?"

"No, they're with Daniel."

"Then let's go celebrate. I want to hear all about the rise of Drew Robbins."

"Oh, Kelly, I'm not sure. I haven't really had a ladies' night out since the fall of Drew Robbins Warren."

"Then I'd say you're due. I will not take no for an answer. We live sixty miles apart, and if I'm willing to drive to your part of town, then we are going out and enjoying ourselves until dawn!"

"Well, now I know who should've been the lawyer. You argue a strong case. Let's do it. It would feel great to get dolled up and actually go out."

I've always felt nervous about letting my hair down in public. I do still feel insecure about going out alone. I guess if it's ladies' night, then neither one of us would bring a man along. Kelly's been with the same man since she was sixteen years old, and they're still going strong. Maybe some men are born to be one-woman men; too bad mine wasn't.

I started to feel excited about venturing out. What if I did meet somebody? I don't know; I'm a mess, but I am human. I would love to find a young, successful, extremely attractive man just to show Daniel I still had it. I knew it would be wrong to use somebody, but I guess with all of the empowering circumstances I'd had lately, I was feeling a little cocky.

It was early in the day, and Kelly had said she would come over around six o'clock. I knew we would have a drink before going out, so I wanted to run to the store to pick up a bottle of wine. I'm not a heavy drinker by any means; in fact, my tolerance is quite low. But I do like to indulge in a glass of wine every now and then. It's actually been more now than then with the stress of the separation and divorce.

Kelly called, wanting to let me know that she had taken care of business at home with her family and was on her way. Because we live so far apart, and planned on being out late, Kelly was going to spend the night with me. She always feels guilty whenever she spends time away from her three children, but I think it's healthy for her to get a break every now and then. I think absence makes people realize how they really feel about each other, which makes the reunion that much better.

The doorbell rang. "Kelly! I'm so happy to see you," I exclaimed, hugging her.

"Drew, you look absolutely wonderful."

"Oh, yes, it's called the divorce diet. But there is one problem: it takes pounds off the body, but adds years to the face."

Kelly and I chatted over a glass of wine, laughed, and shed a few tears. This night was about something positive; we were celebrating life and the changes we had overcome in our lives. At around eight thirty, we decided to meander to a local sports bar.

As Kelly and I entered the bar, I felt out of place. I mean, I was there to enjoy life, not to look for a sure thing with some man I had never met. Kelly told me to relax. She said I needed a drink to unwind.

We sat down at one of the tables near the bar. The place was crowded, so we were lucky to get a seat. The bar was in a smoke-free town, so the air was clear, but the noise level must have been at the highest decibel possible before actually rupturing eardrums. I could barely hear myself think.

The waitress came over to take our order. I indulged in my favorite drink: a White Russian. Kelly was the designated driver, so she ordered an apple martini and a Diet Coke. She said she would be good, and sipped her martini slowly.

Over the next couple of drinks, I confided in Kelly about how I had been slowly piecing myself back together again. It was therapeutic to cleanse my mind of the obsessive thoughts I had been replaying in my head. Kelly was great. She sat quietly and patiently, listening to me talk about the conclusions I had arrived at after countless hours of reflection. I told Kelly that I had finally accepted myself as an individual, rather than a disgruntled partner in the business of marriage where I had been let go. I wasn't sure if Kelly quietly listened to me because she had never been in my shoes, or if she knew I just needed to say everything out loud to clear the slate. Whatever her reasoning, it was working.

From a distance, I heard a loud voice. "Kelly! It's me, Mackenzie!"

"Mackenzie Allen! How are you? I haven't seen you in what seems like forever."

An old friend of Kelly's happened to be there, and I could tell Kelly was happy to see her friend. She asked me if I minded if she sat with Mckenzie for just a moment to play catch-up. I was actually feeling pretty good, working on my third White Russian, so I encouraged Kelly to go reminisce with her friend.

No sooner did Kelly walk away than an extremely attractive, extremely young-looking man approached me. He asked if anyone was sitting in the chair next to me.

"No, please, have a seat."

"I saw your friend leave, and I thought you might want some company."

I immediately knew by the confidence this man exuded that he was a smooth operator, or as my kids would say, a player. But to be perfectly honest, I loved the attention, so I gladly welcomed him.

"What's your name?" he asked.

"Drew, what's yours?"

"Wiggins, Jesse Wiggins."

Okay, as cheesy as it might sound, to paraphrase Rick Springfield, I wanted to be Jesse's girl—even if only for one night.

"So, Jesse Wiggins, what type of work do you do?"

"I'm an educator," he said with a laugh like none I'd heard before.

Consumed by his short, dark hair and chocolate-brown eyes, I jokingly said, "Well, I wondered what the teacher was going to look like this year."

"Good one, although I think I've heard it before."

Amazingly enough, this man was not only sexy but intelligent, too: a rare combination. After exchanging a few stories, I had learned that my newfound educator not only molded the minds of our future leaders but also coached boys' baseball. I thought, what a beautiful man.

It was getting late. Kelly came back over to the table, giving me an impressed look while looking at Jesse, then myself. I impulsively asked Jesse if he wanted to come back to my place for a drink. A drink, as if I hadn't had enough; I really just wanted to enjoy his company for a while longer.

Jesse followed Kelly's car back to my place. Before we made it home, I asked Kelly if she thought I was doing the wrong thing. She assured me that I was a single woman and not committing any crimes, and that I deserved to have a little fun from time to time. I felt a sense of guilt come over me momentarily; however, I was able to suppress those feelings because the excitement of spending more time with Jesse seemed to outweigh them.

We arrived home sooner than I'd expected. Without a word, Kelly immediately walked upstairs, went into Rachael's room, and didn't emerge again that night. I led Jesse into my bedroom. By habit, I turned on the television. I was nervous. I had not been intimate with any man besides Daniel since I was twenty-two years old. We didn't speak. The only noise in the room was coming from the television, which was turned down low. Jesse began to gently kiss my neck. He caressed my body in such a seductive way that I knew he was an experienced lover.

I wanted to be receptive and let Jesse know he was pleasing me, so I began to kiss and touch him, too. Before I knew it, we were undressing each other. To my relief, Jesse had brought protection.

I immediately wondered if he had already planned on having sex that night. The thought passed quickly as we continued exploring each others' bodies. Becoming aroused to an almost climactic point, we began making passionate love. It was intense. When it was over, I laid there thinking that Jesse was now lying in the very spot where Daniel had once lay after we made love. Although it was a depressing thought, I couldn't help but feel satisfied to be lying next to the hot, young teacher. He really was all about performing a service, and I can vouch that the service he provided was of the highest caliber.

Still, I had a hard time sleeping. As Jesse lay next to me, I didn't know if he wanted to stay the rest of the night, or run away. Jesse turned his back toward me, and I began softly scratching his back. He said, "Oh, baby, that feels so nice."

I didn't respond, but I continued to express my gratitude for the outstanding performance he'd given. My body was still trembling; I think it was the aftershock from being with a man truly schooled in the art of lovemaking. As I was scratching his back, I began seriously thinking about how Jesse could have become a master in this art. I figured he was probably a hands-on type of learner. As they say, practice makes perfect; well, Jesse must have had lots of practice. I felt as though I should write him a reference in the morning.

Jesse began to snore, ever so softly. I was glad he was able to fall asleep in my bed. I dozed off and on, perhaps filled with some anxiety as to how Jesse was going to make his exit in the morning. Would he even try to get my number, or would he be up-front about what last night was about?

Around sunrise, Jesse began stirring. I woke when I felt him get out of bed. I looked at his beautiful body as he dressed, knowing I would never see him again. A reasonably large black tattoo, resembling a Bodhi tree of some sort, caught my eye; it was located on his left shoulder. I couldn't believe I'd slept with this man, and I didn't even know the significance behind this tattoo.

He turned towards me, looked me in the eyes, and said, "Good morning, baby. I have a million things to take care of today, so I've really got to run."

I quickly grabbed my dressing gown from the chaise lounge near my bed. I wrapped myself with it, gave Jesse a hug, and told him thank you for a great evening. And just like in the movies, Jesse flashed a devilish smile and smoothly walked away. I had the impression he had played this role before, perhaps many times. As he walked through the threshold of the door, he said, "See ya."

What in the hell was that? He'd talked to me like a buddy or something. I wasn't expecting a scene from some old southern film, but I guess a melancholy farewell would have been memorable, in a good way.

As I stood in my room, I heard the front door open and close. I ran to the window to see Jesse drive away in his shiny, dark blue SUV. I laid on the bed and cried softly. I knew there was nothing constructive about having a one-night stand. Although I had been making personal progress by gaining more confidence in myself and obtaining more control over my life, I felt as though this self-destructive act had made me regress as an empowered woman.

"Drew, are you crying?" Kelly asked with concern as she entered my bedroom.

"Oh, Kelly, what was I thinking?"

Kelly sat on the edge of my bed. I told her about Jesse's casual exit. Although the night had been quite passionate, I supposed that Jesse's effortless attempt to at least pretend to want to see me again outweighed the physical experience. I felt cheap. I also didn't want to think about the number of women he had probably entertained between the sheets, never to see again. I was just another notch on the proverbial bedpost. But then again, I knew I hadn't brought him home to marry him either.

Being a supportive friend, Kelly reassured me that this one-night stand was not a setback, but more a vehicle to narrow my focus and reach my goal of evolving into the whole woman I once was. Packing her overnight bag, Kelly returned to her family, leaving me home alone until the bewitching hour of six o'clock, when Daniel and Julie would bring my children home.

After Kelly left, I made myself a hot cup of tea and sat at the kitchen table. I was exhausted from a restless night, and I'm sure the amount of alcohol I consumed the night before was probably a contributing factor to my throbbing headache. My sheets were in the dryer, and the dishwasher was running. Resting for a few moments, I was thinking about what I should wear for the upcoming show I would put on for Daniel. Then, like a bolt of lightning, I realized that I was being ridiculous. I could not continue this façade. I was a normal woman who had to clean house, do grocery shopping, and fold laundry. Times do occur when I don't look like I just walked out of a salon. Today was just going to be one of those days. I don't look like I just crawled out of hole, but I do have the respect and pride now to look like a woman who is properly maintaining her home and successfully accomplishing the chores that need to be done. I felt liberated.

Chapter 11

I woke up excited about my upcoming outing with Leah. I wanted to get her out into the fresh air and away from the dark, dreary apartment that she seemed to hover in all day long. I thought that perhaps having her away from the safety of her familiar environment would open her up and allow her to reveal more of her past to me. I had gotten to know Leah pretty well over the past few months, but I wanted to know more. I needed to understand how it was okay for her to live the way she was living. I thought it might help me to understand more about people in general. I wanted to understand how some people truly feel when they are living alone and without much money or education. I also wanted to know what circumstances might have caused her to get into this situation in the first place. This was something that my ex-husband would never have wanted to take the time to do. He had made up his mind about "those people" and would never have even concerned himself with the whys or hows of their situation. I, on the other hand, was looking forward to making these discoveries.

The drive over to Leah's was a pleasant one. It was strange to me to think that not long ago I'd hated the thought of driving alone. I was so used to the kids being with me in the car and driving back and forth, here and there. Once they started going with their father on the weekends, I hated the empty feeling I got when I traveled anywhere alone. I would do anything to break the silence: turn on the radio, talk on my cell phone, or roll the windows down to hear the traffic. Now, I embrace the silence. I am no longer afraid to be alone. I enjoy thinking and planning my day. This was just another example of how far I had come.

Although it was February, Georgia weather was as totally unpredictable as usual. It was supposedly going to be a mild, sunny day. I packed a picnic lunch and planned to take Leah to the park to sit on a blanket and share some thoughts. I arrived at her apartment around noon. I was greeted by several of the neighbors who had gotten to know me from my frequent visits. I remembered to bring Rachael's old, pink, stuffed bunny for Jazmine, the four-year-old girl who lived next door to Leah. I'd also baked a sweet potato pie for Gladys. She always came out when she heard a car pull up in the parking lot. It was if she were the "town greeter." I loved to make her smile. She had the type of smile that went from one ear to the other. I wish I could have known her when she was a teenager; I bet she was a lot of fun. As I was handing out the goodies to the neighbors, Leah came out wearing a cute, blue maternity dress. She was really showing now.

"Leah, that dress is just adorable," I told her truthfully.

"Thank you. Gladys sewed it for me last week," Leah said as she turned toward Gladys with a smile.

"Aw, it was nothing," answered Gladys. "I've had the material for years. I knew it would be for something special, just didn't know what." Gladys turned and gave Leah a wink.

Leah and I said good-bye to the neighbors and began our thirty-minute drive to the park. Leah was unusually chatty today. She talked all about her last doctor's appointment, and how she was really having trouble thinking of a name for her baby.

"Oh, it'll come to you," I said reassuringly. "Once you see that little angel's face, you will know right away."

"I bet you're right. I just hope it's healthy. That's all I really care about," said Leah. I smiled to think that she was speaking like a true mother now, and in a matter of months, she really would be one.

We arrived at the park shortly after twelve thirty and were both getting hungry. We walked a short distance before setting up our blanket next to a patch of wildflowers and flat grass. The pond was sparkling with flecks of sunshine, like the flashing glitter of diamonds. There was a light breeze blowing, and it brought us the smell of damp grass. As I began to open up the picnic basket, I couldn't help giggling as I watched Leah struggle to get into a sitting position with her pregnant belly fighting her all the way. I got out the sandwiches, drinks, and fruit and set them out for the taking.

"Wow, this looks wonderful!" Leah exclaimed.

"I thought I would pack something healthy for you and the baby. Plus, it wouldn't hurt me to try to eat a little better myself. Won't be long now until spring is arriving and next thing you know, bathing suits."

"It's hard for me to think about this summer," Leah said with a tone of disappointment. "I mean, I am excited for the baby and all, I just feel weird about not having anyone with me to share this happy time."

"I'll be here for you Leah. I hope you know that," I said, a bit concerned.

"Yeah, I know that, Drew. It's just that—I mean, you have your own family. I just wish I had family, too. You don't really know how lucky you are."

"Leah, what actually happened to you and your family? I know you mentioned your grandmother dying, but what about your parents? You don't need to answer my questions if you don't want to, but I'm really curious."

"I don't mind talking about it," Leah explained. "I just don't like sounding like I'm complaining, that's all. I always hate to hear about people's bad times. It just brings everybody down."

I began to tell Leah how I actually wanted to know about her. How did all this happen? What was she like as a child? Little did I know, her story would not only open my eyes to a different perspective, but also would scar a piece of my heart forever.

Leah began her story, and I listened. I was listening so intently, it was as if she was taking me back in time with her. I was drawn in and there was no way out.

"When I was born, my mama was fifteen years old. She and my daddy were boyfriend and girlfriend in high school. My grandma was so mad at my mama for getting pregnant that she kicked her out of the house. For a little while, we lived with my daddy's parents. Then my daddy decided to go into the army because he didn't have money for school or anything. His parents said they didn't have enough money to raise my mama and me, so we had to leave. My mama was left alone to decide what to do. So that's where it began, the constant moving around like gypsies. She took me wherever she went. She would move from place to place, boyfriend to boyfriend, kicked out of this house and then that one. I think she was drinking and running wild, and nobody she stayed with could handle it. This went on until I was about five or six. Finally, my daddy got out of the army and wanted to see me. He could never find my mama because she was always moving around. My daddy settled somewhere in some small town far away, and my mama would send me on a train to see my daddy once in a while. I was all by myself on a train, probably only about seven or eight. Seemed like hours and hours until I would get there. I remember I could see my daddy's house from the train right before I would get off at his stop. I was so happy because he would always be standing on his porch, holding a bunch of wildflowers in one hand and waving like a maniac with the other. I could always count on him to be waiting for me with those flowers. In fact, these flowers right here reminded me of those times. I guess my daddy couldn't afford much, so wildflowers were something he could always give me. He made me feel so special, so pretty. I told my mama once that I wanted to live with Daddy, and she went crazy! Yelling and hollering. I wish I'd never said that because after that time, I never saw my daddy again."

A tear began to roll down her cheek as she just stared at the patch of wildflowers next to the blanket. I felt a hard, sharp lump form in my throat. I just wanted to hug Leah and tell her I was sorry. But I didn't. I'm not sure why, but I would go on to regret not hugging her.

"What about your grandmother, your mom's mom? Didn't you say you lived with her before you met Rick?"

"Yes, in fact, that whole story I told you was the one my grandmother told me. Don't know if it's all true or not, but that's all I've got to go by. My mama finally had nowhere else to go, and she turned to her mama. We went there with the clothes on our backs, and my mama begged her mama for help. At this point, I was about nine years old and had been in seven different schools.

I didn't even know what grade I was supposed to be in. All I know is that my life was so crazy, so hectic. I had no friends, no home, no toys, no clothes, nothing. It was just me and my crazy mama who made me feel like I was the cause of all her problems. My daddy never made me feel that way. He made me feel like I made all his problems go away."

At this point, Leah stopped and rubbed her tummy. She smiled and took my hand and put it on her stomach.

"Do you feel it?" Leah asked with a smile. "It's kicking me." Leah looked back at her hand as it rested on her belly and said softly, "I am never going make you feel like you're a problem. You're going be the best thing that has ever happened to me, my little angel."

As I witnessed this emotion from Leah to her baby, it astounded me. How is it possible that someone who has lived a life without love can find it in her heart to give so much love away? Perhaps the few years of short visits to her father had actually given her some experience with love and trust. At one point, I'd thought I was going to be the one person who believed in Leah, but I realized she might already have someone. Maybe her father was longing to reconnect with her.

"Leah," I asked, "why didn't your father try to contact you once you moved in with your grandmother? Didn't he know her address or her name or anything?"

"Oh, my granny hated my daddy. She blamed him for running off to join the army and leaving my mama alone to raise me. She told me that my daddy tried to come one time, and she met him in the driveway with a shotgun. He never came back. Then she told me he went off and got married and had some other kids and didn't want anything to do with me anymore, so I just let it be. I know she had to be lying because I never heard that story before, or ever since, but I didn't want to make Granny mad and get me and Mama kicked out. We would be back to living like gypsies again. At least with Granny we were living in the same house, and I was going to the same school. In fact, I loved school. It was the only place I felt normal. I didn't look normal with my cheap clothes and all, but I loved my teachers. They always seemed happy to see me. I even made a few friends. I didn't want to do something bad and get kicked out, so I was always really good in school. I did all my homework and listened to the teachers."

"That's great, Leah," I told her with a smile. "Your granny and your mother must have been proud of you for that," I said hopefully, trying to eke out some type of normalcy in her mother.

"You would think so," Leah said, shaking her head. "Mama didn't even know what was going on at that point. She started staying out all hours of the night. Sometimes she would be gone for days at a time. Then it got to the point where I only saw her once or twice a year. My granny was mad every time she came around. I would just sit on the steps in the morning, wondering why she left me. Then it happened. My worst fear. I was lying in bed one rainy night when I heard a car pull up in the driveway. I looked out the window and saw the sheriff's car. I didn't even get out of bed to see what it was. I just knew. Granny told me the next morning at breakfast. Mama was driving drunk late that night and ran off the road. They said she died instantly. The worst part about it was that Granny didn't even cry. She just sent me to school like normal and told me to be strong. There was no funeral. It was just like one day Mama was there, and the next day she wasn't. That was it. I hated Granny for that, and from then on, we really didn't even speak much."

"Well, I don't blame you," I agreed. "How long did you stay living there with your granny?"

"I stayed until she died, when I was sixteen Even though I was miserable, I stayed. I don't know why I stayed. I guess it was the most stable thing I had, and I didn't want to give it up."

This last statement hit me like a ton of bricks. Leah, staying with her grandmother, lonely and miserable, just for the sake of stability, sounded all too familiar to me. I think maybe that's why I stayed with Daniel all of those years. Even though Leah's life and my life were drastically different, we were connected in many ways. It seems that everyone needs to feel like they belong somewhere, even if that somewhere is a dead end.

"Leah, I know that losing your mother and your grandmother must have been horrible. You were too young to have to deal with all of that. It just doesn't seem fair," I said with a heavy heart.

"You know the really strange part was that Granny did have a funeral, and I never showed up. I couldn't do it after the way she treated my mama. I just couldn't go. She just let my mama die with no recognition of her life—how could I give any to hers? I just didn't go. Soon after that, I met Rick. He wasn't good, but he was better. That was all I needed at the time. Better."

I could tell that Leah was finished: finished with her story, the memories, and the gut-wrenching details of her childhood. She seemed almost relieved to have gotten all of that off her chest and into the open air. I was extremely honored to have been the one to whom she felt comfortable confiding. I realized how special this young girl was and how lucky I was to have the opportunity to be here for her.

"Well, Leah, you are no longer settling for just better," I told her. "You have a baby coming, and you are only going to settle for the best. We are both only going to settle for the best. We're going to start by finding your father. For some reason, I feel that he has something to say about all of this. I am going to help you, I promise."

Leah clenched her heart with one hand, gently placed her other hand over mine, looked me in the eyes, and softly thanked me. She then told me that I was a gift, unexpectedly sent from heaven. I heard the sincerity in her voice, and I told her, in return, that her friendship was an unforeseen gift during a hard time in my life.

We finished up the day touring the park and talking about much lighter things. We talked about the foods we love and the music that makes us feel happy. We rode the train around the mountain and watched the tourists, trying to guess where they came from by looking at the clothes they were wearing. We seemed to talk and talk without a single lull in our conversation. This continued all the way back to Leah's apartment at the end of our day. As Leah began to undo her seat belt, I promised her I would start researching some of the facts she had given me about her father and the few things she could piece together from her memories of the times she went to visit him. Leah was overjoyed with the idea of somehow meeting her father. Before she got out of the car, she reached over and gave me a hug.

As I drove off towards my home, I had some quiet time to reflect on the day. So much had happened, much more than I bargained for. Before that day, I'd thought of Leah as someone who'd made a lot of bad choices in her life. I thought she was a person who needed help making logical decisions. But in reality, I learned that she was a survivor. A person who was making it in a world that failed her. She was much braver than I was in many respects. The day turned out to be so much more than I could have imagined. The reality of it was that I expected to end the day with a feeling of sympathy towards Leah. Surprisingly, however, I felt inspired by her. At one time, I couldn't imagine Leah rising from the ashes to live productively with her baby, but I could see I had been wrong. I felt an overwhelming sense of pride; I was proud to be a woman. I realized we were strong, confident warriors who face demons with different, yet familiar faces. I knew that meeting Leah was no accident. We were meant to help each other.

Chapter 12

Lying in bed recalling Leah's childhood memories of the visits she had with her father, I just knew I was on the verge of a breakthrough to revealing where he lived. Leah mentioned a train practically running through his backyard, and listening to the train's horn blow throughout the night. Was this information the key to discovering the location? I also kept thinking about how Leah said her daddy was poor, so when they would go to the dog races, he could never bet, but it was their tradition to yell for Spunky, the rabbit.

It was almost midnight, but I got out of bed and went straight for my laptop. I was so eager to help Leah. For some reason, I thought I should search rabbits named Spunky. I clicked, and there it was. The first response was titled *Here's Spunky: Dillonvale Dog Races.* Could this be it? I then searched Dillonvale. I discovered it was an old, small town in Ohio possessing several train routes due to the overwhelming number of coal mines. I knew I'd hit the jackpot. Upon further searches, I located an address in Dillonvale for a David Cline, hopefully Leah's father. I printed the address. I searched for more information, but nothing else was revealed. I could not wait to tell Leah that we possibly had her father's address.

Once Rachael and Justin were off to school, I called Leah, and being the early bird that she is, she answered on the first ring. I told her I was stopping to pick up breakfast, and I was calling to see if she had a craving for something special. I decided not to get her hopes up over the telephone about finding an address for a David Cline. I wanted to speak with Leah face-to-face. Leah had the mentality of an abused woman. She had a difficult time expressing herself and what she really wanted. I wanted to tell her in person that we had a possible lead on her father's whereabouts; that way, I'd be able to see her reaction and know for sure if this was something she really wanted to pursue.

As I stepped onto Leah's porch, she immediately opened the door. Apparently, Leah was watching out the window for me.

"Good morning!" I always tried to sound especially upbeat for Leah and her unborn baby. I knew Leah was stressed about her lifestyle and future, so I always wanted to go the extra mile to appear hopeful.

"There is something different about you today," Leah said in a suspicious way. "You meet a man or something?"

"No, Leah, I don't need a man to make me happy. I am actually quite optimistic and happy this morning because of you!"

"Me? What did I do?"

Sitting on Leah's faded denim couch, eating our breakfast off our laps, I slowly began to explain how I found an address for a man with the same name as her father: David Cline. I tried to contain my excitement, primarily because I didn't know if this was actually Leah's father. Suddenly, Leah genuinely began to shed tears of joy. I started to cry as well. I was overwhelmed to see her respond as if she were being rescued from an eternally doomed life. I guess it had been a long time since I had experienced witnessing a lost soul discovering hope and having the expectation of a chance at a normal life.

I asked Leah what step she wanted to take next with this information. She didn't know, so I suggested that we write a letter verifying that he was her father.

"I'm scared. I want to write a letter, but what if he doesn't write back, or if he really doesn't love me anymore?"

Without thinking, I impulsively said, "Of course your father loves you. We'll do this together. You have nothing to lose and everything to gain."

At this stage of the game, I knew I had to follow through and make Leah's dream a reality. I told her there was no time like the present, and we needed to begin our correspondence today. I wanted to be home before the children got off of the bus, but that was several hours away. We always seemed to do our visiting at Leah's house; we rarely visited at mine. I felt uncomfortable bringing her to my house because she might feel intimidated or insecure. Besides, I liked to have a change of scenery, and although her home was a bit depressing, Leah always made me feel welcome.

Leah and I took a trip to a nearby drug store to buy some stationery. I wanted this experience to be special. Because there was an age difference between the two of us and because I identified Leah as a lost soul, I felt like I mothered her at times rather than only offering her my friendship.

Leah picked out some stationery with a floral print because she said her father used to tell her that princesses always had flowers. Leah then retold me her fondest memory of how her father would stand in his backyard holding flowers as she would pass by on the train when she was coming to visit. After she passed him standing in his backyard, he would meet her at the train depot near his home, and then he would give his princess the flowers.

As soon as we arrived back at Leah's, we sat at her kitchen table that was an old, off-balance card table that sat four. Sitting in a dinged and dented metal folding chair, I asked her what she wanted to say to her father.

When Leah began speaking, I listened intently because she seemed to have a difficult time expressing herself. I knew Leah's father would understand her scattered thoughts and ideas, so I wanted to make sure I captured the messages Leah wanted to convey to him. I think Leah's emotional state, being pregnant and not exactly living on easy street, made it more difficult for her to think clearly.

"Do you want to see your dad again? Do you want him to read your letter and contact you? Do you want your dad to know you are expecting a baby?"

"Yes, Drew! I want all of those things. I want to be with my daddy, and I want this baby to know him and love him like I do. I'm just scared. I don't know what to think or what to wish for. This might not even be him."

I confidently looked into Leah's eyes and said, "We are going to make your heart whole again, and I am going to walk with you hand in hand until you are with your father. I will not abandon you or mislead you. I promise, Leah, you have my word. You're not alone."

I told Leah to take the paper and pen, and I began to dictate the letter to her. Inspired by Leah's love for her father, I had her begin the letter by stating that she was writing this with the intent of finding her long lost father, a man named David Cline, who had a daughter with a woman named Melody. This daughter, Leah, was born in 1989 in East Point, Georgia. Then Leah independently started to write from her heart. She wrote how she loved her father and was confused by the current situation of not knowing where he was or why they were not together. She ended the letter by asking him to respond if this was in fact her father. Leah included her address on the outside and inside of the envelope. She did not want to pressure him into contacting her right away, but of course Leah's reality was skewed, and she could imagine him visiting her the very next week.

We placed a stamp on the letter, and dropped it in the mailbox. What would fate bring us? I said my good-byes and headed back to the house so I would be home before the school bus dropped off my kids.

I did some light housecleaning while I was waiting for the children to arrive. I felt uplifted because the ball was finally rolling for Leah, and I was excited to see Rachael and Justin.

"Mom!" Rachael called out.

Walking out from the kitchen, I could see the excitement stamped across Rachael's face. "You look like you had a great day," I said. "What's happened?"

Justin followed behind Rachael. Closing the front door, Justin said, "Yes, your majesty, tell Mom the good news."

"You got the part in the play!" I exclaimed.

Rachael and I embraced. I told her how proud I was of her. Justin gave a few words of encouragement as well. Rachael and I had been up a few late nights rehearsing for the lead role in the school's spring play. Although I knew Rachael was talented, her school was so big, I knew there was bound to be competition.

"Let's celebrate! Rachael, we'll go to the restaurant of your choice. I want to hear every detail from the tryouts to the posting of parts."

Sighing, Justin said, "Oh, great, this is going to be a long dinner."

"Oh, Justin, give your sister a break. Besides, I want to hear about your day, too."

Soon, we were off to eat a tasty meal at a local Indian restaurant. I was struck by how the memories flood your mind sometimes. Before the breakup, Daniel would take us to a variety of Indian restaurants around town for dinner. We even ate at a not-so-authentic Indian restaurant when we vacationed in Germany one summer.

I only wanted to concentrate on the children and their successes, not my obtrusive memories of Daniel and the past. Sitting with the children, I laughed and watched them interact with me and each other. I admired them for their ability to bounce back from some hard emotional times and move forward in life. I patted myself on the back a bit for not revealing the feelings of resentment that I still held for their father. I never wanted to burden the children with my hostile feelings. It took an overwhelming amount of willpower to maintain a stable lifestyle and a healthy environment for the children during some depressing, dark months.

After a beautiful evening with Rachael and Justin, we arrived home in time to finish homework, bathe, and pack for school the next day. I briefly spoke with Kelly in between running bathwater and packing lunches. Kelly knew me like a book. We were the kind of friends who told each other everything. We never had to impress each other, or pretend we were something that we weren't. We were vulnerable and honest with each other. I was so happy when I spoke with her because I'd had such a powerful bonding time with the children. They renew my spirit, and Kelly is always encouraging and motivating. Perhaps mutual feelings of love between my children and friends are all I really need. It was unconditional love at its best.

A couple weeks had passed since Leah and I mailed the letter to David Cline in Ohio. Leah was feeling discouraged. I told Leah about one time when I had mailed a Father's Day card to my father, and he received it three years later. A person was committing fraud, and my father's card had been collected for evidence. It was strange but true. I suggested we write another letter, in the event the first one was lost, damaged, or caught in the side of some mail container. Anything was possible.

In case the David Cline we wrote to was Leah's biological father and was still mulling over the first letter, I told Leah writing a second letter couldn't hurt. Again we sat down and addressed the concern of not knowing why communication had stopped between the two of them. Leah mentioned a few personal thoughts and updates. I suggested she not unravel her whole life story, in the event this David was not her father, although I made it clear to Leah that I really did think he was.

This letter was sent sixteen days after the original letter. Leah seemed to be obsessing over her father and what she thought his reaction to the letters would be. I think she was really counting on him to be this superman kind of father who would swoop her up and change her life forever. Maybe he would. I did pray, for Leah's sanity, that her father would respond to her letters.

As I was consumed with finding Leah's father, I needed to pull myself away and devote some time to a large account I was given at work. I dreaded showing my face around the office, but I knew I had to let the bosses see me working diligently. After all, cutting through the red tape is what it takes to get you where you want to go in a company, and I had to do what they wanted me to do. In a way, knowing how to play the game determines professional success. I am a strong woman. I continued giving myself silent, motivational pep talks in the elevator on my way up to the office. I may be insecure in other aspects of my life, but if there is one thing I am confident in, it's work.

I walked out of the elevator like I owned the place. I greeted the receptionist and everyone else I walked passed. With my head held high, I embraced the knowledge that I was a powerful woman who had goals to meet. Secretly sweating and hoping not to have to have an awkward, impersonal conversation with Mr. Rankquish or his associates, I casually walked into my office and gently closed the door.

Taking a deep breath, I thanked my lucky stars that I knew how to put on a brave front. I guess I have Daniel to thank for that. After a sigh of relief, I got down to business. I had a multimillion dollar account with a pharmaceutical company who wanted me to advertise their newest product. The wonder drug, about to hit the market, was a quick fix for every depressed person on earth. I felt like I could have been the poster child for the product.

After putting in about seven long hours, with no breaks, I felt a sense of accomplishment, so I started to clear my desk and pack my bag. I heard a soft knock at the door.

"Come in."

Jack slowly opened the door. "Drew, good to—oh, are you leaving?"

"Hello, Jack. Yes, my work here is done for the day. I think the pharmaceutical company will be quite pleased with the progress. You know how passionate I am about my work."

"Will I be seeing you soon?"

"Of course, I'm pitching for another top-dollar account for a children's boutique next week. You may be seeing me so often in the near future, it'll be like old times."

"Well, then I look forward to our next encounter. Enjoy the rest of your day."

I couldn't help but be cordial to Jack. We had a history, and as much as I felt slighted by him, my professionalism won out; I had to show him respect.

Driving home, I replayed my pitch for the boutique, just to keep my mind occupied. While at a red light, two young teens caught my eye in the car ahead of me. Young love: innocence and naïveté. At the rate I'm going, I thought, Justin will experience love before I do. I had to laugh to myself when I had these thoughts. There are moments when I feel lonely and long for companionship, but then I think about the package that accompanies the companionship—less personal freedom, more compromising, pushy in-laws—and my desires seem to dissipate.

Later that evening, Leah called. Saddened by not hearing from her father, she was desperate to go to the address we were sending the letters to. After calming her down, I was able to talk her into allowing me to travel with her to Ohio, but only after we sent one more letter. It seemed to make Leah feel better to know that we had a plan B if this David Cline did not write back.

The next morning, I arrived at Leah's home to help her write a final letter. This time, the letter revealed that this would be her last attempt to contact the man she thought was her father. The letter went into great detail about how Leah remembered her father standing in his backyard, waiting for the train to pass by while holding flowers in his hand. Leah wrote about how she would be so excited to see her father while she passed on the train. Their eyes would meet, and their souls would connect. Picking Leah up at the train depot was magical. Her father would give the flowers to her and Leah would curtsy.

I provided Leah with the details as to when I would be able to accompany her to Ohio. I could never allow a woman who was eight months pregnant to travel independently, let alone a friend. Selfishly, I knew I wanted to make myself busy when the children would be on vacation with their father in March. I gave Leah the specific date and time we would be passing by the mystery address.

Including this information in the letter, Leah informed her father that if he wished to communicate with her, he should stand in the backyard holding a flower. This would be the signal letting Leah know he wanted to see her and talk with her. If she did not see him in the backyard, then Leah would continue on the train until she reached a nearby city.

I mailed the letter on my way home. I told Leah since we were not going to go to Ohio until March, we were giving him plenty of time to write back. All I knew was that I needed to go home and start packing for my birthday trip back home to visit my parents. The children and I could use a trip.

Chapter 13

Finally, vacation is here. Traveling to visit my parents is always a special time. They still live in the same house in which I grew up, in a small town in Virginia. It is a wooded lot way back from the main road, very private and peaceful. My parents have been married for forty years and are still very much in love. My mother had the traditional role of stay-at-home mom who cooked, baked, and cleaned. She was very involved in my school and is still very involved with the community: a true inspiration. My father is a biology professor at the local college and is also an inspiration to many people. His ideas about nature and the earth almost take one back to Native American folklore. Although he is not so much a religious man by nature, he is very spiritual. He is also a man of few words. He would much rather be sitting on his porch, listening to the sound of birds chirping than to be chatting on the phone engaging in meaningless conversation. Although his words are few, they are words of meaning and merit. I did and still do cherish every one.

Growing up, I was always my daddy's girl. We would spend many afternoons hiking and talking. He would point out things to me along the way that most people would never recognize: a bird's nest nestled in the brush, a salamander egg sack in a pond, or a foxhole near the foot of a tree. I always felt that the two of us were the only ones who recognized such things; it was our little secret. That is why the phone call I made to my father a year ago was so difficult. I still remember like it was yesterday.

"Daddy, Daniel and I are getting a divorce." There was silence on his end, and I was just wondering what words he was going to speak to me this time. Did I let him down? Was he no longer proud of me? Was he somehow going to believe I failed and that this was my fault?

"Drew," he said in a very soothing manner, "I am so proud of you for hanging in as long as you have. Your mom and I recognized problems years ago. You have always been too good for him. Now, when are you and the kids coming to visit?"

I was so relieved to know that he seemed the same as always. It was just what I needed to hear. No questions asked, no inquisitions, just trust in me. He felt sure that I knew what I was doing. I could tell it by the tone of his voice. My mother, on the other hand, reacted the same way any mother would probably react. She wanted to "kill" Daniel. Of course this was entirely his fault and how dare he do this to the kids? I needed to hear that side of it, too. Unconditional love. The same as I have for my children and always will.

Rachael, Justin, and I arrived at the house around six p.m. We greeted one another with big hugs and the sound of laughter from Mom. There was also the overwhelming smell of something delicious wafting out from the kitchen. Mom took the kids into the den to give them their surprises, and I immediately went upstairs to my room. As I opened the door, I noticed the lavender paint on the walls and a brass bed, which now seemed so tiny, in the corner. Just as I had left it. I lied down on my bed and looked over at the fuzzy pink phone that sat on the dresser. All the memories of my teenage years came flooding back: lying on this bed, talking on the phone to my friends, making plans for the weekend. I also remembered keeping a journal and writing here, in this very spot, filling the pages with all my hopes, dreams, and aspirations. Tears welled up in my eyes as I began to remember the innocence of that era. How the world was once my oyster and I was so confident. Nothing could stand in my way. I laughed to think of how I lost that part of me while I was married, like many women probably do. It made me reconnect with the fact that I really was a whole person before I was married. I really liked myself then.

Recently, after meeting Leah, I began to feel what I thought was a newfound confidence. But actually, I have really just begun a journey back in time to a place where I used to be. A place where all I needed was the love and support of my family and the love I had for myself. I guess seeing how Leah faces the world so much on her own, and yet seems to make the most of it, really makes me admire her as person. She is not afraid to be alone. In fact, she once told me that sometimes she would rather be by herself because she is the only person she can trust. In some ways, I believe what she was saying was that she is her own best friend. I kind of like that thought. I love my children, family, and friends, but what is wrong with loving myself? It was liberating for me to think of starting this new chapter in my life. Taking control of my feelings and fulfilling my dreams will be my next step. I can't believe how much I have changed in just one year. The newly divorced me would have been home alone on my birthday, thinking of the children and their fabulous skiing trip with Daniel and

Julie. The new me is here, with the people I care about the most, celebrating my life. I am still so proud to have confronted Daniel about this vacation and my being with the children. I realize how much I admire myself and the way I have handled such a difficult situation. I have heard it said before that a man is judged not by how far he falls, but how high he climbs back after the fall. I have proven to myself that, no matter what happens, this woman will stay true to herself.

My thoughts were interrupted by a gentle knock on the door. "Come in!" I said with a bit of laughter, seeing as how this wasn't really my room anymore.

"Drew," Dad said as he stood at the door looking in, "it is so good to have you here. I am so proud of you and the way you have raised two such respectable, intelligent children. I always knew you would turn out this way."

"Well, I had the best teacher available," I said lovingly.

"If you don't mind, I'm going to take the kids on a little adventure hike in the back woods. Seems like we have a pheasant's nest behind the bushes back there."

"Have fun, Daddy. I'll go help Mom in the kitchen. And Dad, just so you know, I am proud of me, too. I have you and Mom to thank for that. Thanks for everything." We looked each other in the eye for about five seconds. Nothing else needed to be said.

As the kids followed Dad into the woods, they looked like two little cygnets following their papa cob. I didn't know who was more excited, Dad or the kids. I went to the kitchen to help Mom get ready for dinner.

"It smells so good in here," I told Mom lovingly.

"Well, I am making your favorite meal, chicken and biscuits. After all, it is your birthday," she said with a wink.

"There is no place I would rather be right now than home with you and Dad. The kids are so excited to be here," I said wholeheartedly.

"Well, it is better for the kids to be here with us than with that homewrecker Julie on some dangerous ski slope in the middle of nowhere. Does Daniel not realize how dangerous skiing is? It's as though he has really lost his mind," Mom said with a face full of anger.

I began to peel the skin off the potatoes and place them in a bowl for mashing. "Mom, don't be so hard on him. Just let it go," I told her in a surprisingly non-bitter tone. "Let's talk about something else. When do you and Dad want to come to the lake house?"

"Well, Dad is thinking about retiring this year, so I believe we would have quite a lot of time next summer. Will work allow you to take off?"

"Ugh," I sighed. "I don't even want to think about work right now."

"You know, Drew, your father and I believe that you need to start your own company. It is really hard for women to get ahead in a place that is run by men. You're smart enough to do this on your own. You don't need to ride on the coattails of anyone else," Mom said firmly.

I thought about what she'd just said, and I began to get butterflies in my stomach. Why hadn't I thought of this before? I am sure that some of the women who were still working at the firm would gladly come my way. All I would need to do is get enough money to rent my own place. That wouldn't be hard. I could start renting out the lake house for profit. Just then I realized Mom was staring at me is if there was smoke coming from my ears.

"Gotcha thinking, didn't I?" she said, smirking.

"Yes, Mom, you have. Right now I'm in the middle of a big proposal, but after that, things may be heading in a new direction," I told her.

"Well, you know Dad and I are here to support you. You can even move in here with the kids if you need help getting things started." Mom has wanted us to move closer for years.

"No, Mom, we will never move in. Perhaps closer, but never that close," I said as I went over and hugged her tight.

We chatted for a time until Dad came back with the kids. They all smelled like the woods and were so anxious to tell us everything they saw. Dad just sat back and listened, as he always did. He never felt like he had to be the storyteller. He was just the one who allowed the stories to be created.

Dinner was wonderful. We talked and laughed about old times. Mom and I sipped on a bottle of wine and giggled as Justin did impressions of his teacher, Mrs. Grimly. Even Rachael laughed so hard she spit out a bit of her drink.

We ended with a beautiful birthday cake and everyone sang to me in such out of tune voices it made the hairs stand up on my neck. I opened a few gifts and then we retreated to the den for a movie. Both Justin and Rachael fell asleep on the floor next to the fire. Mom, Dad, and I moved into the living room for some coffee and a little more visiting.

"So what is new with you, Drew?" Dad asked.

"Well, there is a new situation with Leah, the girl you met at church." I continued to tell my parents the whole story: the confrontation with Rick, our picnic in the park, and our letters to the man we hope is Leah's father.

"Oh, Drew," my mother began, "you have to pursue this. You could change this whole girl's life."

"I know," I told them. "But in a weird way she has really changed mine."

"How do you mean?" Dad asked.

"Well, when I first met Leah, I was broken. I felt as if I had failed my marriage, my kids, and myself. I was jealous of Daniel and Julie and of everyone else who had it better than me. I felt inferior to my neighbors and my friends at the tennis club. Everyone was gossiping about us, and the children were teased about it. Things were bad. Then I met Leah. She has so much strength and courage. She is a fighter. I would go to her apartment, which was in a very poor part of town, and nobody judged me there. No one gossiped about me or cared about my personal situation. They were just friendly. Everyone had problems there, yet they were open and honest about them all. No one was trying to pretend they were something they weren't. Leah showed me that all I really need is to be confident and to surround myself with people who are not vindictive. It has just been an eye-opening experience for me. I am ashamed of how I used to judge people like Leah and turn my nose up at them. What I should have been doing is taking the time to get to know them. I could have learned something valuable about how people are to be treated in the world."

My dad smiled, and then Mom asked, "If you find her father, are you going to go with her to meet him?"

"Yes," I replied. "We have plans to go next month."

Mom sighed and said, "All a person needs in life is to know that somebody believes in them. Stick with it, Drew. You are going to be her angel. I can already tell."

Dad laughed and said, "Well, I think this angel is getting tired. I need to go to bed so I can get ready for another day of adventure with the kids. I thought we could go to the Nature Center tomorrow if that's okay."

"Sounds great, Dad, we wouldn't miss it for anything." Dad always had a way of bringing us all back to reality.

We finished our conversation and decided to turn in for the night. It felt great to know that my parents were supporting me in every facet of my life. Mom was right. If every person had just one person who believed in them, this world would be a better place. I am going to be that person for Leah. I was actually excited to think of my return home to Georgia and helping Leah. Also, having a new outlook on my career and all of the planning I would be doing was inspiring me. I am on a mission, and once again, nothing can stand in my way.

Chapter 14

I am spent. Who would have known that carrying around this tiny baby would drain me of my energy to the point of exhaustion? I feel like I'm sleeping my life away, but the doctor said it was normal, and that my energy would pick back up again. At least all of this resting has given me more time to think. I have been thinking a lot about my past. I've been thinking about how I got to this point in my life. When I try to think about all of those days and nights I spent with Rick over the last two years, it's hard to remember; somehow, those memories seem to be fading. They are being flooded with my new hopes and dreams for my baby. Although Rick will probably never completely disappear from my mind, his existence will become a distant memory.

Unfortunately, I already wonder how and when I will tell my angel about Rick. Although I will make a safe, loving home for this baby, I know there will come a day when my child will probably want to know about his or her father. Rick was a man who once made me the happiest person in the world. When he was good, it was great, but when he was bad, he hurt me deeply. All those scars he left on my heart and in my mind nearly broke me.

I knew I deserved better than the occasional bone he threw me when there wasn't a better offer. I get down on myself for letting it go on for so long, but I was holding out for him to discover how much he loved me. But that day never came. One thing I know for sure, Rick may not have been any Prince Charming, but in the end, he has given me the greatest gift that anyone could have given me, and that is this baby growing inside me. I already love this baby unconditionally. All of these experiences I have endured have given me direction in life, and it has motivated me to set high expectations for my child. My goal is to be the best mother possible. I know what a precious gift this baby is, and I will sacrifice whatever it takes to provide a stable life for my angel.

Before Drew went out of town, she asked me something that's been wearing on my mind. She asked me how I was going to support the baby and myself once the baby was born. I've been praying for a long time for the Lord to help me to know the answer to that very question. I have been asking myself over the past months: What am I good at? What are my talents? What could I do? One afternoon, it finally came to me. While lying on the couch, thinking about the ever so near future, my eyes drifted to my sewing machine. A feeling of awe came over me; I knew I had my answer. Tears filled my eyes. If there was one thing I could do, and do right, it was sew. I started to get excited. Images of purses, aprons, blankets, and all sorts of gifts raced through my mind. Thinking of holiday crowds and accepting orders for personalized gifts for friends and family made me think back to my childhood.

We didn't have much money, but I remember once, before Christmas, Mama took me to the mall. My mama and I were walking around when I saw the most beautiful stand with all kinds of handmade bags and embroidered gifts. Mama kept walking, but I stopped to look at the merchandise. There was a magnificent sign above the stand that read "Torrie's Treasures." I wished I had every treasure there. Torrie looked so happy talking with her customers. Like it was yesterday, I remember picking up a quilted, embroidered bag with my actual initials on it; I pressed it against my face. The soft material felt like a pillow, and I could smell a light scent of flowers. Torrie asked me if I needed any help, and I said no; then the next thing I knew, Mama yanked my arm so hard, it nearly came out of the socket. Mama was not happy to discover me missing from her side. I was never able to get anything from that stand, and I never saw Torrie's Treasures again.

Years later, here I am finding myself making the decision to begin a career at making my own handmade treasures. I could work from home with my baby, and find a store to sell my gifts. I'm not naïve; I know there are lots of details I'd need to iron out before this dream could be made into a reality, but I'm glad to at least know the direction I need to move in. Drew will be happy when I tell her of my plans. She will be proud of me, too, and she'll help me get to where I want to be with this idea. Like Drew tells me, all I have to do is ask. I think Drew doesn't want to over-step any boundaries by automatically doing things for me, like a mother would for her child, but I know she likes to make sure I have what I need and that I'm in a good situation.

Although Drew has made the comment to me from time to time about how I have such a positive outlook on life, she has been my saving grace. Drew has shown me how a mother expresses love and concern for her children, yet at the same time maintains her own identity. Although Drew is cultured and doesn't have money problems, she is a lot like me. She hurts when she's sad and laughs when she's happy. I don't think that she and I are so different. With her wisdom and experience in life, Drew has been a driving force for me to reclaim my self-esteem and strive to set goals. Drew is a motivated person; she achieves successes in life because she is smart, and she sets examples for Rachael and Justin with her strong work ethic. I have learned so much by listening and watching Drew. She is selfless. She has been a mentor to me. The impact she has made in my life has changed me forever. I wonder if I will ever get to repay her for her friendship, or if I will ever make as great an impact on someone else's life as she has on mine.

I sometimes think about what kinds of things my old classmates are doing, or who could be impacting their lives. What do eighteen-year-olds do? I bet not many of them are planning for a baby. I bet some of them are making decisions about what to wear to a party or which beach to go to during a semester break. I wonder if Robbie has a girlfriend. If so, I bet she's pretty.

My life has not been a run-of-the-mill type of story, but considering the hoops I've jumped through, to have a place of my own and still have the fuel in me to light a fire, I'm not doing so badly. I have those desires to live the American dream; I'm just not taking the typical route to get there. Sure, I think about falling in love with a man who kisses me goodnight and kisses me good morning, a man who is smart and funny. But my priorities are set; I've got to have this baby and take care of it first. True love can wait. If the Lord wants me to have a husband one day, then so be it. I gladly accept my fate. I'm not going to do anything to rush it or ruin it.

Chapter 15

There's nothing like returning home after a much deserved vacation. Rachael's play was the next main event.

Practicing day and night, for six consecutive days, repeating line after line, was all we did. We ate, drank, and slept the play. But it was worth it.

I was lying in bed the night before the play, when Rachael crawled in next to me and asked me if I thought she was ready to perform. I told her if she wasn't, then I was. I reassured her that she knew every line, that I knew every line, that our furniture even knew every line. Rachael laughed. I let her sleep in my room; I wanted her to get a fantastic night's rest so she would be in the best of moods tomorrow for the show.

Sitting in the auditorium, Justin read the playbill, and I anxiously sat, watching families and friends pour into the room. Daniel caught my eye, and I impulsively waved him and Julie over. I immediately said to Justin, "You should sit next to your father, too."

Taking the high road was never easy. In the back of my mind, I wondered if I was crazy. Then I patted myself on the back and said I'd file it as good karma.

As they approached, I said, "Daniel, you and Julie come sit with us. Rachael will be so happy to be able to look out and see her family together."

"Thank you, Drew," Julie said with confidence, yet a dash of humility.

"Son, I haven't heard the long version of your trip to Virginia. Go on any hikes with your old Pop?

I turned away to give Justin and Daniel some semi-private father-son time before the curtain call. I could still hear Justin speaking to Daniel, but I couldn't catch Daniel's responses. I could tell Justin was excited to share details from our trip. I wondered if Daniel felt jealous hearing about the fun they had without him. I personally don't like to think of the children making wonderful memories without me, but that's really a selfish issue I need to overcome.

The lights flickered. I said a silent prayer for my baby girl, and then the show started.

Rachael was on cue in every instant, and she looked absolutely beautiful. She was the only fourth grader in the entire play. At one point in the play, she wore a satiny, glacier blue ballerina dress with black stitching. She looked like a porcelain doll with her ruby red lipstick, blond hair pulled up in a tight bun, and her perfect posture.

Tears fell from my eyes because the talent she exuded was unbelievable. I was extremely proud of my daughter. The hard work and late nights were well worth the outcome. I saw Daniel lean over toward Julie several times during the show and make comments. I knew he was proud, too. Although Daniel was a letdown as a husband, he did love the children.

When the play was over, Rachael met us in the atrium. Julie and I each had a bouquet of flowers to give to Rachael. We awkwardly took pictures of Rachael and Justin with each parent, and then one with the five of us. I felt like I was in an after school special in which we'd all live happily ever after.

At any rate, Daniel, Julie, Justin, and I praised Rachael's performance. Then I guess Daniel wanted to show me how he could take the high road, too, so he invited us out to dinner. It was getting late, but it seemed like one of those nights on which you don't really want the momentum to end, so I graciously said we'd love to. Again, I thought, wow, I bet I'm collecting enough karma for an entire year.

Dinner was interesting to say the least. My goal was to get through the meal without asking Julie how it felt to be the cause of my divorce. No, I knew she wasn't the only culprit; it was just easy to point the finger at her. If anything, I wanted the children to see that their father and I had a civil relationship and respected each other enough to move past the pain and recover from the anger and sadness. If I didn't allow myself to evolve into the classy, intelligent woman that I was, how could I ever expect my children to learn from my mistakes?

The children were upbeat and quite talkative during dinner. When the meal was over, we said our good-byes, the children hugged their father, gave Julie a wave, and then we went home. While riding back to the house, Rachael said she had a perfect night. Hoping she was talking about the dinner, as well as the play, I asked her what made it so perfect.

"I love tonight because my family was together, and Julie was there, too."

I had never really asked either Rachael or Justin about Julie, because I never really wanted to know. I was afraid to ask, but the next words out of my mouth just escaped with no warning.

"Do you love Julie?" I had to know. I secretly felt threatened by her. I never spoke about her with the children because I didn't want to mention her name, or inspire the children to think about her. Giving her any credit for nice things she had done for my children or for their father was definitely never going to be easy for me. I know that sounds harsh, but honestly, I may forgive, but I can't forget. I'm human; I'm not perfect.

"Well, kind of, but not like you or Dad. Julie is fun and she dresses cool, but she is not my mother."

Then Justin said, "We love you. Dad loves Julie, and we hang out with her because she's with Dad."

Suddenly I felt silly for never having asked the kids about Julie before. I know my children are loyal to me, but that doesn't mean they can't have other relationships throughout their lives.

"Well," I replied, "I love you two with all of my heart."

As I pulled into my driveway, I noticed some of my old friends gathered outside a neighbor's front yard, the mothers of the girls who had been taunting my children on the bus. I pulled my car into the garage and told the children to go inside to get ready for bed. I had an agenda of my own. I proceeded to walk across the street to confront them. They quickly turned to me with their fake smiles and asked how the kids and I were "hanging on."

"Better than ever," I told them. The women looked surprised. "Yeah, throwing Daniel out was the best thing I have ever done for myself. You see, when I saw how you all behave—you know, being subservient to your husbands and turning to malicious gossip as a means of entertainment—I realized that I wanted to be a real person. A person of substance. Basically, the total opposite of all of you." I felt almost entirely satisfied, but I wanted one last dig. "By the way, Cynthia, your tennis playing really sucks."

I heard the ladies gasp, and I turned toward my house so they wouldn't see me smile. I know that was seriously immature, but I had had enough of the relentless bad-mouthing these women had been doing in front of their children. Their gossip had affected my children, and I wouldn't stand for that. I'd had enough from the neighbors, enough from the smug men at the office, and enough from Daniel.

The next morning I was hoping to catch up on some sleep, but the phone rang just after eight. I answered it on the first ring, trying to prevent the children from waking up. It was Mr. Rankquish's personal secretary, Mia, a sweet, young Chinese woman. I sat straight up in bed, and my stomach sank; Mia has never called me. Mia was normally cheerful and at times even silly, yet she knew when things needed to be done, how the orders needed to be carried out, and she was never late on any dead-lines. Mia complemented Jack because of her positive, carefree demeanor.

I asked Mia if there was a problem at work. She was not herself as she calmly explained that there had been an accident the night before, involving Jack. I was taken aback and felt overwhelmed with anxiety.

"Mia, talk to me! What about Jack? Where is he?"

Almost incoherent, I heard, "He tried, but he, he didn't—"

"He tried what? Did he hit somebody?"

"He didn't make it."

There was silence. Neither one of us spoke. I was at a loss for words. Mia and Jack were strictly professional, but sometimes, when you work closely with somebody for an extended amount of time, you form a bond, like family. I told Mia that I was very sorry and to please let me know when the arrangements had been made. She asked me not to call Jack's wife, Maria, because she was still in shock. Of course, I told her, I would honor her request, but if there was anything I could do, I would gladly lend a hand.

How fast our perspective on life can change. After hanging up the phone, I thought to myself, I have so much. My life is enriched with my loving children; we have our health, and we have limitless opportunities in life. I was shocked that Jack was gone. He would miss his daughter's wedding, grandchildren, and so many moments and highlights in life. I was sad for Maria. She will never again be kissed or comforted by her husband. Jack cherished his wife, and they had a marriage based on love, which is rare.

The next day, I called my parents to inform them of Jack's death. Since my parents and I were close, they knew the relationship Jack and I had when I first started working for him. I think I was more affected by how quickly life can be taken away, rather than the actual accident itself. Honestly, Jack and I were not as close as we once were. But being exposed to a death demands a thorough reality check, and sometimes we discover that some changes need to be made in our lives to make us better people. Life's too short to allow our shortcomings to prevent limitless opportunities.

Mia called me later that evening with the funeral arrangements. She was composed enough to expand upon Jack's accident. I didn't want to ask her, but I was curious. Apparently, Mia and Jack were at the office working diligently on legal documents that needed to be overnighted to a client whose potential high-dollar account could actually impact our company stock. Mia could complete the paperwork with her eyes closed. Jack was exhausted. He had been under a fair amount of stress to meet certain deadlines. He was a workhorse; he thrived on setting high standards for his employees, and he lived up to those standards himself.

Jack was so tired, with glassy eyes and a headache coming on, that he began making errors, so Mia persuaded him to go home. It was approaching nine o'clock. Mia guaranteed Jack that she would finish the work, and mail the documents that night. There wasn't much left, a few seals and a few self-addressed envelopes and the job was complete.

Taking Mia up on her offer, Jack set out for home. There were witnesses who said they saw a silver, two-door convertible BMW pass by with a male driver slumped over the wheel. The police report revealed that Jack had fallen asleep at the wheel and veered off the road, hitting a tree and dying on impact. Jack only lived eight miles from work. In a matter of minutes after pulling out of the parking lot, Jack was dead.

Mia was the first person called. The police found Jack's cell phone in his mangled car and contacted the last person called. Jack had called Mia to thank her for her dedication and for pushing him out of the office.

Mia immediately left work and drove to Jack and Maria's home to speak with Maria face-to-face. Jack had often spoken of Mia to Maria, and the women were genuine friends. Maria was like a mother hen to all of the employees. She did not approve of any funny business, no cutthroat competition or talking behind people's backs. She was a woman with dignity and pride. Maria was as ethical as they come, and if you wanted the honest-to-goodness truth, then Maria was the one to ask. She was a gorgeous Irish woman; she would always joke about her little pixie-styled hair possessing every color in the rainbow. Maria stood about five feet tall, but she always wore heels that gave her at least two more inches in height. One time I saw Maria wearing denim overalls, but usually she wore dresses that matched her shoes that matched her earrings that matched her necklace. I admire any woman who could look that good and maintain a grounded attitude. Jack was successful, but Maria came from old money. They were a lovely couple. Mia and Maria sobbed together.

While the children were in school on Monday, I solemnly paid my respects to Jack's family and close friends. The casket was closed; Jack's body was severely marred in the accident. There was a handpainted family portrait resting on a stand next to his casket. As I stared intently at the smiling faces, I reflected upon the idea that they would never be a whole family again. But then I thought, they must continue their lives, cherishing memories of their father, or husband, and accept him as a guiding spirit of some sort. Through the pain, they will persevere. The children will grow, change, and as the world spins, we will face new challenges and rich rewards every day.

On Tuesday, I made the decision to have the children miss school in order to attend Jack's funeral. I felt as if the children were old enough to experience the closure of a life. Although the children only vaguely remembered Jack, I thought that, in their sheltered lives, it would be important to expose them to a harsh reality. But we would be together, and they would witness genuine people affected by death.

As ironic as it sounds, death is really the only permanent situation that occurs in life. That means, as living creatures, we really do have choices and decisions we can accept or deny. I want Rachael and Justin to realize that life is what they make of it, and we should be grateful for the blessings bestowed upon us in our daily lives. Although my broken heart has mended to a degree, in the grand scheme of things, my love life is minute when compared to war and bona fide tragedies.

A photographic slideshow was displayed before the eulogy. I had never observed such a tradition. It was actually quite beautiful; the visual photographs and music that accompanied the memories were touching. Justin was teary-eyed. I felt that he was probably moved in a private way, so I refrained from asking him what was making him emotional.

Following the funeral, we proceeded to the cemetery. Father Victor read from the Bible. He told a story about how when he was a child, he played football at Saint Maria Christina High. One day, he was going to start in a varsity game. Father Victor was so nervous. During the school day, he replayed the plays he would implement and the strategic ways he was going to be the hero for the mighty Bulldogs. Well, fifth period came around, and he was offered a couple of Jordan almonds. He graciously accepted the snack and, in his anxious, excited mood, popped them into his mouth. Well, the rest of the day unraveled in an unexpected way. The day ended with one almond cracking a tooth, an emergency trip to the dentist, and no playtime in the game. In fact, Father Victor never even made it to the game due to an unexpected reaction to the Novocain used at the dentist's office.

The point of Father Victor's story was that no matter how much you prepare or hope for a situation to occur, God has a plan for us. The plan may not coincide with our desires, but we must accept events we encounter, whether we understand them or not. Father closed with a prayer. The children and I said our good-byes and returned home. The children were quiet and subdued in the car.

Chapter 16

After a good night's sleep, I woke with such clarity as to what direction I wanted to pursue in life. Although I had emotionally healed by leaps and bounds, my heart still ached for Daniel. I guess having once believed we would never part, accepting reality was a struggle. Waking up alone was difficult, yet I was a woman with integrity, and if I planned to get Daniel back, I would only be shortchanging myself. Realizing this, through many discussions with Kelly, over time, the truth was beginning to sink in. Denial plays funny tricks on a person, but reality has to dominate in the end if the result is to be a healthy one.

I needed to get up and feed the children before they caught the bus for school. I was excited to begin my day because I wanted to visit with Leah. In fact, I volunteered to take her for her prenatal checkup. We were going to find out the gender of her baby.

On the way over to Leah's home, I heard a song on the radio that reminded me of my high school days. It lifted my spirits and gave me a sense of security. I was confident back then, and, listening to that old music, I felt my old self resurfacing again. I knew time was what I needed, accompanied, of course, by the support of my family and friends.

Upon arriving at Leah's, my cell phone rang. A previous client was returning my call. I had called him impulsively the day I returned from Virginia. My parents had so built me up to go after running my own advertisement agency that I called Jacob James, a renowned businessman, for advice on how to go about opening a business. I answered the phone.

"Good morning, Jake."

"Drew, it's so good to hear your voice. How are you?"

"Wonderful, and how are you on this fine morning?"

"I'm doing quite well. I know you called a while ago—please accept my apology for not getting back to you sooner. I was in New York City for a conference, and then visiting family in Schenectady."

"Oh, Jake, no apology is necessary. I was actually calling you for a selfish reason. I'm contemplating opening up my own business, and I was calling the guru himself for business advice."

"That's wonderful, Drew. I didn't think it made sense for you to be a part-timer," Jake said with a laugh.

"I know you probably have a full schedule, but would you be able to fit me in sometime in this millennium?"

"I think I can do that. I'm in the car now, but I'll check my schedule once I get to the office, and I'll give you a ring back later today."

"Sounds perfect. I appreciate your time. Thank you, Jake."

"Looking forward to speaking with you again, Drew. Good-bye."

"Good-bye, Jake."

Before I could jump for joy, Leah already had the front door open and was giving me a curious look.

"I'm coming, Leah, hold your horses," I said with a smile.

"Who were you talking to? A man?"

"Yes, it was a gentleman, but we were discussing business."

Leah grabbed her purse, and then we were off to the doctor's.

"Are you excited?" I asked Leah. Although I was still excited about Jake calling me back, I was excited for Leah, too. I remember finding out the gender of both of my babies.

"Yes! I am excited. I hope I don't cry. I just want this baby to be healthy. I want to love it and take care of it."

"I know you do, Leah. You already love your baby."

We didn't speak for the rest of the ride; we were both probably daydreaming at opposite ends of the spectrum. Leah's doctor was located in a sketchy part of town, but everybody was nice there. It was a doctor's office that accepted government-funded insurance. The exterior of the building was made of bricks that had been painted white perhaps twenty years ago. Weeds were growing between the cracks in the sidewalk and bordering the building. It looked as if the businesses or stores around the doctor's office were run-down or vacated. I didn't like Leah going there alone. At any rate, I was glad to share this experience with her today.

Watching the baby on the ultrasound brought tears to my eyes. Leah repeatedly asked, "What is it?"

The doctor turned away from the screen and looked Leah directly in the eyes and said, "Be patient, your daughter finally stretched out."

"Leah, you're having a girl!" I congratulated her immediately.

Leah was overwhelmed with excitement and joy; she was speechless. After the shock wore off, Leah was in rare form. It was as if she wanted to pick her daughter's name by the end of the car ride home. Leah was obsessing over names and what her baby was going to be like and look like. It was actually inspiring to listen to her thinking aloud, bouncing ideas off me about the baby. Even though Leah was broke and did not necessarily have a sound and secure future, she spoke as if none of those factors mattered or existed.

I dropped Leah off at her house after the doctor's office. Gladys was sweeping the front porch when I pulled up. I waved hello to Gladys, and good-bye to Leah as she stopped to talk with Gladys. I could hear her sharing the exciting news as I pulled away.

Daydreaming about opening up my own business, I could not help but think about my conversation with Jake. He and I have a professional relationship, but there was something alluring in his voice when I spoke to him today. I had never had feelings for him in the past. What had changed? I thought. Was it that I have changed? All I knew was that I was looking forward to his next phone call, and our upcoming encounter.

Rachael and Justin returned home at the usual time. I had prepared an early dinner because Rachael was singing, along with her classmates, at the PTA meeting that night. Over eggplant parmesan and pasta salad, I explained to the children my idea of pursuing my entrepreneurship in advertising. They were encouraging and thought it was a fantastic idea. I also filled them in on Jake. I told the children how I was waiting for his phone call, and that he would help to point me in the right direction. Justin, having worrywart syndrome, asked why I thought Jake had all of the answers. I laughed and told Justin that I had faith in Jake because we had previously worked together, and Jake had had to believe in me first. "Therefore, I am returning the favor," I said jovially.

On our way out the door, the phone rang. I didn't want to be late to the PTA meeting, but I also didn't want to miss Jake's phone call. I quickly answered the phone. It was a telemarketer. I immediately said, "Not interested" and hung up.

The PTA meeting was introduced with the typical speeches from the principal and co-presidents of the association. After the business part was over, the show began. The entire fourth grade was standing, side by side, on the stage and additional risers were necessary to elevate all of the children. I was so proud to watch and listen to Rachael. Glancing around the room, I saw parents I had not seen in a while, even ones whose children were in classes with Justin. Although I was sitting without a husband, I was with my son. With Justin by my side, or the children in my heart, I was never alone.

When the performance was over, we rode home singing the songs from the meeting. Justin had performed those same songs just two short years ago. Their poor music teacher, Miss Casey, taught the same songs to the same grade levels year after year. I guess this was to ensure that she would not have to teach a song that only half the class knew. I would think that this technique must grow tiresome, but then again, some people thrive on routine.

As I was putting the clothes away before bedtime, the phone rang. Thinking it was Daniel calling to check on Rachael's PTA performance, I answered it in a nonchalant manner.

"Drew, did I wake you?"

"Jake, no, how are you?"

"Again, I can't complain. And I apologize for calling so late. What is it, going on nine thirty?"

"No problem. In fact, the children and I attended a PTA function tonight, so we really haven't even been home long."

"Well, I waited so long to call you back because I thought I had a possible cancellation for tomorrow, and I wanted to verify that before setting up a date and time with you six months from now. So, lucky for me, the cancellation was verified, and I'm hoping you're available tomorrow, say around noon?"

"Jake, I think I just cashed in on some of my good karma. Tomorrow would be wonderful."

"Then let me take you to this new sushi bar near my office. We can discuss whatever you'd like. In fact, I could swing by your place on my way back from a morning meeting, and then we could go straight to Roll My Way."

Laughing, I told Jake, "I appreciate it, and I look forward to seeing you tomorrow."

In a gentle, yet manly voice, Jake responded, "Until tomorrow. Goodnight."

"Goodnight, Jake."

Lying in bed, I pondered about Jake. I was feeling a bit excited to meet with him. I really did want business advice, but I found myself daydreaming about Jake, the man, not just Jake, the business advisor. Jake was about five feet ten a nice solid build, and athletic-looking, but still looked like he probably enjoys a few adult beverages on the weekends. With amazing green eyes to complement his brownish-reddish hair, Jake was an attractive man. He had been married once. I didn't know too much about his personal life, but I sure was interested in finding out.

Why am I obsessing over this man all of a sudden? It's not like I've never seen or spoken with a man in my life. I was experiencing feelings I had not had in a very long time. Was this just me having a natural desire for the craving of physical contact with the opposite sex? I would not exactly label myself as a lustful woman; however, there are times when I miss the intimate touch of a man, and the comfort that accompanies sexual satisfaction.

The next morning, when the children were getting ready for school, I told them I would be meeting Jake for lunch to discuss business.

"Yeah, right," Justin mumbled.

"Excuse me?" I paused. "And what is that supposed to mean?" I waited. "Justin."

"What?"

"How dare you give me this attitude this morning?" I turned away from Justin, but then I decided not to just let this go. "I am your mother, and after all of the sacrifices I make, the love I provide, and the care that I give you, you are going to act like this? I would have expected more respect from you."

Quickly, Justin reacted. "What? Do you like him? Rachael and I don't even know him. Why do you seem so excited?"

"Justin, you are obviously missing the point. I am meeting with Jake to discuss business, and if I want to speak with him personally, then as a single, thirty-nine-year-old woman, I will. I encourage you to seize opportunities in life. I do not limit you or your sister. As the sole parent in this household, I deserve to be excited, or happy for that matter, in whatever situations arise for me. Whether there is something that will positively enrich our lives as a family, like me running my own business, or individually, like a relationship, I don't want to hold back. I don't want regrets. You need to accept this. You are acting immature and selfish when you think you can pitch a fit to get your way. I love you, and we are in this together for the long haul."

Soon, the children were off to school. I couldn't help but think about Justin's attitude, but I'd said my piece, so I had to let it go.

I was dressed for success by the time Jake picked me up. Of course I was casually watching out the window for his arrival, but I waited for him to ring the bell. The greeting was nice. I had not seen Jake in such a long time. He looked even better than I remembered. Wearing khaki pants and a thin, olive, argyle sweater, he was worth more than a few daydreams. We shook hands once I opened the door. And Jake immediately complimented me on how well I looked.

Although this was a business luncheon, the gentleman in Jake could not hide; thus, he opened the car door for me and shut it once I was settled. The aroma of his cologne filled the air inside his classic, canary yellow mustang. His car was spotless, and the custom leather interior reinforced the notion that Jake was a successful man who knew what he wanted and knew how to achieve it.

Since I had never ridden in Jake's car before, I acknowledged his classic beauty by telling him how impressive she was.

"Her name is Sandy."

"Sandy? Now there's got to be a story behind that name. Care to share?"

"Her name is Sandy because she gives me chills every time I see her."

We laughed. Jake was funny, yet I think he was being serious.

Arriving at the sushi restaurant, my mind was thinking a million thoughts a minute. I had so many questions for Jake, and I wanted to remember all of his responses. Right off the bat, Jake asked what the ultimate motivator was for me to want to start my own business. Impulsively, I explained how it was a piece of the evolution occurring within myself, a new beginning.

After what had to be a solid hour of business dialogue, I think I exhaled. Jake was so accommodating. We then seemed to drift into personal conversation. Exchanging flirtatious words, we laughed and enjoyed each other's company. We felt comfortable with each other, and Jake's demeanor was soothing. The luncheon abruptly ended when Jake received a phone call from the office. "A pleasurable two-hour lunch had to end at some point," Jake noted.

As Jake walked me to my front door, he again shook my hand and told me how he wished the lunch did not have to end. I reciprocated by telling him how I couldn't remember having a better time than the one we just shared. Briefly, time seemed to stop; for a moment, we were peering into each other's eyes, and then I became bashful and looked away. Jake asked if he could call me for social reasons, not business. I graciously assured him that I would look forward to the call.

As I walked inside the house and closed the door, my mind was racing with romantic thoughts of the future. Realizing I was getting ahead of myself, I tried to reason with the strong desire I had to run after Jake and tell him that I was in love with him. Quickly coming to my senses, I knew I was acting this way because I was sincerely lonely. Loving the children unconditionally and feeling their love for me was not in the same ballpark as being loved by a man or feeling the passion a man has for the woman he cherishes.

Chapter 17

It was probably around two o'clock in the afternoon on a Saturday when Leah called hyperventilating; she threw me into a panic. When I heard her sobbing and struggling to muster the oxygen needed to breathe like a normal human being, my first thought was that she was going into premature labor. After I yelled at Leah to calm down, she was able to explain that she had received a response from her father. I was taken aback, speechless. I mean, this was really something she and I had frequently talked about over the past several months, but I guess it seemed so far in the distance that I did not think about the consequences or benefits of receiving a response.

The letter Leah received confirmed that our David Cline was her father, but more importantly, that he was alive. Leah read the letter to me as she attempted to stop crying. I was in shock. Leah probably read me the letter five times. It wasn't a long letter, but it was rich. David stated in the letter that he missed Leah, had never stopped loving her, and definitely wanted to see her as soon as possible. I said to Leah, "Our trip is on!"

I could not imagine the joy and frustration Leah was experiencing. She had so many questions she wanted to ask her father, but she also had so many dreams she wanted her father to fulfill, beginning with reuniting with him.

Calmly, I told Leah that I would confirm our trip to Ohio on Monday. Just then, Rachael walked into the room and asked, "Where are you going?" I quickly told Leah I was happy for her, and that I would call her back. I hated telling the children about any plans that did not include them, not that there were many. I don't know why, but I felt like I was cheating them out of experiences if I did something without them. As crazy as that sounds, I was still stuck on the children making memories without me, and me making memories that excluded them. They are my world, my priority, and I couldn't help but think of them all of the time.

I turned to Rachael and said, "That was Leah on the phone. She wants to reunite with her Dad. I don't think an eight-months-pregnant woman should travel alone, do you?" I did try to manipulate the decision making, so that Rachael would think she was part of the idea of me traveling with Leah.

"Oh, definitely not. You should go with her in case she has the baby early," Rachael said without a doubt.

"You are so right, Rachael. How did you grow to be so mature?"

We shared a laugh, and then Rachael asked me if we could go to the pet store because she wanted a guinea pig. "A guinea pig?" I said in terror.

"Mom, you know our class pets are guinea pigs. I love them! Can't we at least go and look?"

It's no secret that I am afraid of animals. Yes, me, the daughter of a biologist. My father would live in the rain forest with all of

God's creatures if my mother would let him. But a guinea pig, I knew I could handle, because it lives in a cage, and I could insist that Rachael and Justin keep it away from me.

I called Justin into the room with us. "What's going on, Mom?"

"Your sister wants a guinea pig."

"Okay."

I thought, as if he didn't already know Rachael was going to ask for one. I asked Justin what he thought about having a guinea pig in the house.

"I don't care. Can I get an air gun?"

"Why? Are you going to shoot your sister's guinea pig?"

"No! But if Rachael gets something, can't I?"

What have I raised? When I was a child, I never asked for anything. My good behavior was expected, and I rarely got any extras. To even ask for something was considered rude or disrespectful. Apparently, I'm not raising my children with the same standards, but in actuality I was okay with that, if only because I wanted my children to be nervier than me. I settled for things because I was taught not to question, not to ask for something better.

I guess today was going to be a shopping day. I told Rachael and Justin we would swing by the store to pick up an air gun, if, of course, Justin agreed to abide by my plethora of rules pertaining to the gun, and then we would hit the pet store for the ungodly creature, I mean, guinea pig.

When everything was said and done, we returned home around five o'clock. I needed to make dinner and unwind. I always wished for the days to be longer on the weekends when I had my children. Still struggling with the fact that I had to share my children, I felt depressed at times, but things were getting better.

I didn't want to forget to call Leah. I knew she basically sat home and did nothing when she wasn't working, if I wasn't taking her some place or if Gladys wasn't home. I decided to call her while I was making dinner.

Leah told me that she must have read the letter from her father a million times. She told me that she was studying his handwriting, looking at the envelope he used, wondering about the pen he used to write the letter, and thought about the post office where he mailed the letter. I could understand the excitement, but the obsession was a bit much. I guess this is part of what made Leah and me so different from each other. I am a go-getter type of person, a person who sets goals and strives for success, but Leah pretty much sat around just waiting for something to happen, good or bad. We were products of our environments.

Leah and I chatted for about ten minutes, and I assured her again that I would confirm our plane and train reservations and that in the event she were to change her mind, she and I both would continue on the train and stay in the hotel for a ladies' weekend. I didn't want to upset Leah by expressing the possibility that her father might be some strung out loser, but let's face it, neither one of us knew exactly what the situation was going to be once we arrived.

Time flew over the next couple of days, and soon two weeks had passed. Packing for our trip, I was sad the children were already with Daniel for the weekend, and that I would be traveling without them, but I guess I know that deep down, I cannot stop the world when my flesh and blood are away from me. I knew I only had a few minutes to spare before I had to pick up Leah, and head to the airport, but I desperately needed to hear

Rachael's and Justin's voices. I hesitantly called, the voice mail picked up, and my heart sank. Tears rolled down my cheek; I felt lonely, and I missed my children.

On my way to pick up Leah, I was rethinking the plans and details of our weekend and how it might unravel. Leah was peeking out of the window as I drove up to her home. I saw Gladys sweeping her porch as I approached the driveway. As Leah came tearing out of the house, Gladys tried to say something, but Leah cut her off, saying, "Not now, G, Drew and I are on a schedule and nothing's going get us off track. Tell you all about my trip when I get back. Love ya, G!"

As I'd noticed before, Leah and I were birds of a different feather, but perhaps it was my maternal instinct that drew me towards her. "Are you ready?"

"I've been ready. I couldn't sleep a bit last night. And I've never been on a plane before, so my angel and I are a little scared."

"I bet you are scared, Leah, this will definitely be an adventure neither of us will never forget."

"In a good way or a bad way?"

"Leah! Relax. I would not let anything bad happen to you. Think of me as your guardian angel."

Leah smiled back and then turned her head to face the window. I could see her reflection as she daydreamed about what she hoped the trip would bring. She looked peaceful. It made me happy to see a spark of life from a girl with such a troubled life.

We were almost at the airport when my cell phone rang. Jake was calling.

"Hello, Jake!"

"Drew, how are you on this fine day?"

I grinned from ear to ear and answered, "I'm great. I am actually on my way to the airport with a dear friend for a much anticipated ladies' weekend trip."

"Wow, makes me wish I were a lady sometimes," Jake said with a chuckle. "When will you be returning?"

"We plan to be back in Atlanta late Sunday afternoon."

"Well, once you get settled back in, I'd like to take you to dinner one night. How about I give you a call on Monday to touch base with you?"

"That would be lovely."

"Enjoy your trip, and stay out of trouble."

"Thank you, Jake. Talk with you next week."

As soon as I hung up with Jake, Leah looked at me and said, "I wish I were in love."

Taken aback by her comment, my defense mechanism kicked in and I assured Leah that I was not in love, although I was probably in lust. I emphatically found myself explaining how we were friends who, perhaps, were beginning to express feelings for each other. As if I were talking myself out of the possibility of love, I spoke to Leah as if she were my own child, telling her that two people who do not know each other that well could not possibly be in love. However, deep down, I did want Jake to be in love with me.

Arriving at the airport, going through security, and finally making it to our gate was a trip all on its own. What a nightmare. But I would rather be safe than sorry. The plane ride was smooth, and transitioning from the airport to the train station was a success. Once we were on the train, Leah became extremely anxious. I was afraid she was going to give birth right then and there if she did not calm down.

"Leah, let's just breathe and try to calm ourselves. We have come here for a purpose, you are not alone, and we are here for each other. You have waited, patiently, for this day for so long. Embrace your joy and the love you have for your father. Put your worries to the side—you want your little angel to feel your happiness, not concerns."

"I know you're right, but I can't help it. I'm scared. What am I going to say to my daddy when I see him?"

"Leah, when you see him, you'll know what to say. He's your father—you're his flesh and blood. You will know when you see him. Remember, in the letter he sent you, he said there would be a sign for you to know where he was. He said when you saw the sign, you would know everything was going to be okay, and that you would remember. Do you know what the sign could be?"

"I don't know. I have been thinking about those words over and over again, but I can't think of what kind of sign he could be talking about."

I smiled at Leah and told her that at any rate, we were making this happen, and it would be wonderful.

Riding on the train proved to be an emotional experience like no other. Traveling closer to our destination, I spotted something peculiar from a far distance. I tapped Leah on the shoulder and pointed in the direction of the unknown. Leah began to cry. As we approached the back of some small, run-down, wooden homes, I could not believe what my eyes were fixated on. There was a backyard covered in a blanket of beautiful wildflowers in every color of the rainbow. It was unbelievable. The flowers were at least a half-foot thick in depth. It was the most extravagant sight I had ever seen. I was in awe. Leah wept like a baby with tears of joy and happiness. I looked at Leah and asked, "Is this the sign?" She did not answer. "Leah, is this the sign?" She began to nod her head.

"Remember, Drew, Daddy says princesses deserve flowers."

I was moved. Tears streamed down my face. I was speechless. Leah and I did not exchange any more words until we arrived at the depot. I embraced her once we exited the train. I had arranged to rent a car once we reached Dillonvale. I pulled the directions to David's house out of my purse; it was only a little over two miles away. We silently rode in the car, deep in thought. I reflected upon my own relationships in life, missing Rachael and Justin.

Driving onto a short gravel driveway, we saw David Cline waiting on his small, cement front porch, holding one long-stemmed daisy. The car was still running when Leah bolted from the front seat. I remained in the car. Watching Leah and her father reunite was touching. By the looks of it, I think David had lived a hard life. Although he was younger than me, his life had aged him. David had thin, messy blond hair, his belly hung over his pants, and his skinny legs held him up to be about an inch shorter than Leah. I could tell Leah was his daughter, though, because they both had the same beautiful blue eyes. I gave them some time to be alone; I pretended to be organizing a few items in the car. Leah waved for me to join them.

"Daddy, this is my very best friend. She has looked over me like a mother."

"Hello, sir, I'm Drew."

"It is very nice to meet you, Drew. I feel like I won the lottery today."

David turned toward the house and suggested we go inside. As I happened to glance back at the car, I noticed neighbor children staring in our direction. I wondered if David did not usually receive guests. I even noticed curtains drawn and people watching the reunion. It was strange, but then again, perhaps it was me who was the stranger in this small town.

Epilogue

It turns out Leah's father, David, had received all three letters. He was just unable to read them. David, now thirty-six years old, had never learned to read. He carried the letters in his callused hands down the hot, dusty road to a neighbor to reluctantly ask for help. Sara Lynn, a kind widow who ran the local bakery, answered her door. She saw the look of concern on David's face and asked him in. After giving him a glass of sweet tea, she took the time to sit down with David and read each letter to him. In one of Leah's letters, she mentioned her memory of her father standing in the backyard holding a wildflower in his hand and waving to her as she looked out the train window. "One of my best childhood memories," is how she'd put it. As he listened to these words from his estranged daughter, a tear rolled down his cheek. He was speechless.

"I didn't think she would remember those days," David said as he wiped his eyes on a pink paper napkin.

"Well, David, she did and does. I'm going to help you! Your baby girl is coming, and we are going be ready, you hear?" Sara Lynn said encouragingly.

After Sara Lynn helped David to respond to the last letter stating that he was her father and wanted to see her very much, they got ready. Leah wrote back with the date and time she was coming, and the town took over from there. In fact, at Sunday morning worship, the preacher announced that the town was going to help Mr. Cline prepare for his reunion with his daughter. Everyone clapped and cheered as David sat and wept, his heart overflowing with gratitude. No one asked why he hadn't kept in touch or what the situation was; they all just wanted to help.

The night before Leah's expected arrival, the children of the town were given wheelbarrows and clippers and were told to fill the wheelbarrows to the top with as many wildflowers as they could find. Then they took them and dumped them in his backyard. Sara Lynn opened up the bakery that evening with free cookies and milk to all the kids who helped. It was a real bonding experience for the town. Everyone seemed happy and excited to meet Leah, but none were as anxious as her daddy.

The first meeting with Leah was special. From the moment she walked in the door, she and her daddy hugged and cried. Drew did not feel the need to stay very long. She too cried because she knew Leah was home. She would be safe and feel the sense of belonging that everyone needs. Leah's father walked Drew to the door and simply said, "Thank you for giving me my life back. You are an angel." That was enough spiritual healing for Drew to carry with her for a lifetime.

One year later, Leah went out to check the mail and came back in with a huge smile on her face.

"Daddy, look, a letter from Drew," Leah said to her father as she began opening up the mail on the kitchen table. "Let's go on the porch and read it together."

Leah and her father went out on the porch of her father's home, which they now shared. Leah sat on the porch swing with baby Angel in her lap as she began to read Drew's letter to her father. She had been teaching him to read, so she read the letter slowly, pointing to each word as David looked over her shoulder:

> *Dear Leah,*
>
> *How are you? I cannot wait to come and see you this summer for Angel's first birthday. It seems as though you and your father are doing such a wonderful job raising her. The pictures you sent me were just precious. Angel is growing up so fast!*
>
> *What a difference a year makes. My kids are doing very well. Both are thriving in school and have really seemed to come into their own this past year. I have just finished my third month of running my own advertising agency. I am excited to tell you that I was able to hit the ground running. I kept some of my old clients and got referrals for many others. It is so wonderful to be working full-time and loving it. I am the only one I have to answer to, and it can't get any better than that.*
>
> *Jake and I are still dating. It has been such a wonderful experience. I have never felt this level of contentment. Everything is progressing so nicely with the two of us. I have a feeling that you, too, will be experiencing this type of connection, or should I say reconnection? That is so amazing that after all this time, you had the courage to write to your high school crush, Robbie! And to think he is coming to visit you during his next school break. That is wonderful! Please fill me in on all the details as soon as possible!*

Also, I went by to visit Gladys the other day, and I showed her the baby pictures you sent me. She giggled and brought out some of her own stash that you had already sent her! I am so happy you two have stayed in touch. She seems to really miss you, but she is doing well. I believe she will be moving in with her daughter soon to help raise her grandson, and she is really looking forward to that opportunity. I told her about your new business venture, and she was ecstatic! Gladys feels, as I do, that your talent for making handbags, blankets, and aprons will make you very successful. Sarah Lynn will also benefit with the sales. Making her bakery into a bakery/craft store was ingenious. I will be stopping in to see your shop when we come to visit you this summer.

I would really like to take this time to thank you, Leah. All that time I spent with you last year really helped me to grow as a person. Seeing your strength and honesty gave me the ability to rediscover my own. I knew I had it in me—I just had to find it. You are an inspiration to me, and I know you will be to Angel as well. Give her a kiss for me, and I will see you in a few months.

Love,

Drew

Leah closed the letter and gently kissed Angel on the head as a small tear rolled down her cheek.

"She is a good friend, isn't she, darling?" Leah's father asked.

"Yes, Daddy, one of the best I have ever known," answered Leah in a very soft voice. This was how she was now most of the time now, soft-spoken and tender. Many in the town noticed the change in Leah's heart this past year since she'd been with her father. The community had made her one of their own. She felt loved, and it showed. She and her father were the happiest people in town.

"Daddy, let's go to town and catch the dog race tomorrow. We can bring Angel. She needs to get to know the tradition we have around here," Leah said with a smile.

"Sounds great to me," David said as he reached down, picked a wildflower, and placed it behind Angel's ear.

Meanwhile, miles away from the old coal mining town, Drew was closing up her business for the night. She was turning the key to lock the door of her own office building when she felt a gentle hand on her shoulder.

"Ready to go, sweetie?" Jake asked as he reached for Drew's arm.

"Always ready for dinner with a handsome man like you," Drew said with a seductive smile. They began to walk towards the car when Drew stopped and noticed a small piece of paper the size of a playing card on the ground. As she picked it up she noticed it was a picture; there were no words on it, just a beautiful painting of an angel. Drew chuckled a bit and said under her breath, "I guess they're everywhere."

"What did you say?" Jake asked.

"Oh, nothing," Drew answered as she slid the picture into her pocket. "I'm famished. Let's go eat."

Acknowledgments

To my children, Alli and Jordan, and my husband, Jeff: thank you for giving me the kind of love that has inspired me to be a better person. To my parents: your guidance and support have helped me to fulfill all of my dreams.

Michelle Atha

My aspirations in life are motivated by the unconditional love I have for my children, Bailey and Julianna, and for each and every one of my godchildren. Thank you to Kelly and Daryle for encouraging me to pursue this project.

Meaghan Wagar